I0749686

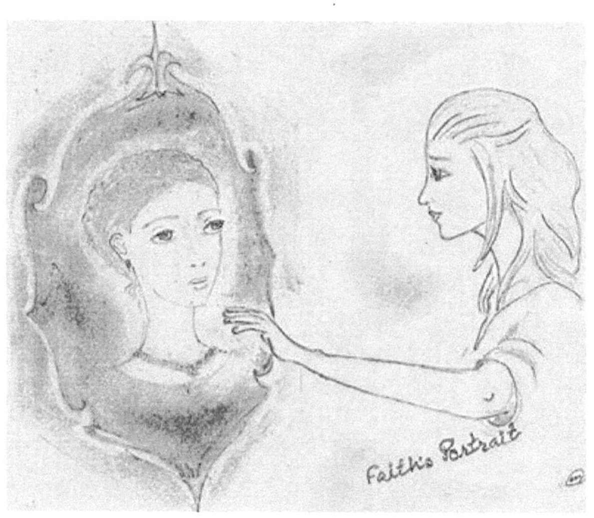
Faith's Portrait

Faith's Portrait

Jude Liebermann

Printed in the U.S.A.
Cover design by Linda Ballard
Sketch by Mouri Ghosh

Published by Lee Books
El Cajon, CA
www.readatleebooks.com

ISBN (paperback) 978-0-9660653-6-7

Chapter 1

She took a wrong turn on her way home from therapy and found the house by accident. Claire Todds stopped the car at the curb and stared at the three-story building. The dilapidated house had obviously not been taken care of, but the "For Rent" sign in the window caught her gaze. She quickly wrote down the phone number listed on the sign and then sat back to stare at the house. A smile broke through her normal austere expression as she gazed at it. As Claire saw herself living there, she finally took note of the surrounding area. The nearest house stood a block away, which ensured utter privacy. A high fence encompassed what looked like a huge back yard from her vantage point. She did frown as she finally noticed all the weeds in the front yard. Claire would definitely have to hire some of the local boys in the neighborhood to help out. She suddenly laughed, already feeling as if the place were hers.

Her mood lifted greatly, Claire pulled away from the house and made her way home. She normally had nothing to be happy about on her way home from the painful ordeal of therapy. Her hips and legs would scream in agony for at least two days afterwards, but she knew it was important. If her parents hadn't made her go to the necessary sessions every week, she might never have regained her ability to walk. She sighed as she remembered the accident.

Claire had been crossing the street when a car made an illegal turn and struck her. Many painful surgeries had followed to repair her crushed hips and legs. She had only been sixteen at the time and even a decade later, she still suffered from the accident. She couldn't even be overly mad at the driver of the car, who had been an old man that claimed he hadn't seen her. Due to his bad vision, he had only lost his license as punishment for the accident. Though she tried not to remember him being more concerned with his expensive BMW than whether or not he had killed her. She couldn't remember much about the accident, but she could never forget him glaring down at her where she lay on the street. At least he had full coverage, so all her medical bills had been taken care of. She still wished someone had the sense to take away his license before that fateful day.

She sighed as she shook her head. "No use crying over spilt milk," Claire muttered to herself as she pulled into the driveway of her parents' house. She had been able to move away from home for several years, but it took time to work up the nerve. Since the accident, her parents spoiled her and hadn't wanted her to live on her own. They always feared that she would fall and be unable to make it to a phone to call for help. Claire would laugh at their silliness. "Nothing's wrong with my arms, you know?" She would always answer.

Claire now sat with the slip of paper in her hands where she had written the phone number. She would call first and see if she could afford the house before telling her parents about it. With a deep sigh she pushed open the car door. Grabbing her cane from the passenger side, she used it and the door to get out of the car. Pain shot through her, and she bit her lip to keep from moaning. The front door opened and her mother raced out.

"Honey, do you need help?"

Claire held up her free hand and shook her head. "No, Mom, I'm OK! Just landed wrong." She finished with a forced smile.

Her mother shook her head and wrung her hands as she watched her daughter limp her way toward her. "You sure, Claire?"

Claire sighed, feeling her joints loosening up a bit. "I'm just a bit tight right now. I'll feel better in a few hours." She spoke the truth after all, since some days she didn't need the cane's assistance. Pain didn't always accompany her noticeable limp. After ten years, she had almost gotten used to the dull throb that constantly plagued her.

"Well, I made a cake…chocolate… your favorite. Would you like me to cut you a slice?"

"Sure, Mom. That sounds great!"

While her mom went into the kitchen, Claire walked into her room. She had been upstairs until the accident, but usually tried to avoid stairs. Her therapist made her use the Stair Master, which she absolutely hated.

She walked over to the phone and dialed the number on the slip of paper. A man answered. "Sam here."

"Oh hi! I'm calling about the house on Elm? Is it still for rent?"

At first she heard nothing but the shuffling sound of paper. "Well, yes it is. Actually it was just listed this morning."

"This morning?" Claire repeated, clearly shocked that she just happened to run across it the very day it listed. "Well, I'm very curious what the rent is."

"Eight hundred a month."

Claire gasped. "For that mansion?"

Sam chuckled on the other end. "Well, I wouldn't call it a mansion. Might have been back in the day, but…well, you saw it. It hasn't been taken care of and is a bit of a fixer upper. I'm actually surprised the owners aren't trying to sell it instead of renting."

"I'll take it." She said quickly.

"Well, how about that. I'll just need you to come into the office and fill out the paperwork, then Miss…?"

"Oh, Todds…Claire Todds." Her happiness made it very hard to concentrate on the rest of what he said, but she wrote down the address of his office, made an appointment and then hung up the phone. Her hand still rested on the receiver, when her mother came into her room.

"Did you make a call, dear?" She asked, the slice of cake in her hand.

Claire nodded, the smile slowly fading. Now she had to tell her parents.

All her family and friends came out for the move. They had her packed and transported over as soon as her application went through, and she signed the lease. She had been pleased to learn of the basement, which made a perfect location for her dark room. Photography had always been her passion, and she made a good living from it as well. Some of her photos had even made it into national magazines.

Claire did as much as she could, but for the most part just stayed in one place and unpacked things. Her friends helped clean up the downstairs. No one did much with either of the upstairs floors, since they felt she wouldn't be spending any time up there. Her parents had been shocked to see the house their daughter had rented. They just couldn't understand why their crippled daughter would want a three-story house. She tried to explain that her therapist had been pushing for her to use stairs more often, as that would work out her legs and hips more. Just going down to the basement would surely help out, though she couldn't wait to explore the entire house. The pain of her recent therapy session had mostly faded, and the excitement of the move made her feel more than up for the task.

As her parents attacked the lawn, and her best friend put things away in her new bedroom, Claire made her way down to the basement. She cringed the entire way and sighed as she reached the bottom. She smiled to see that someone had already cleared away the cobwebs and left the boxes of her photo gear on the worktable. They had even put up a clothesline that spanned the width of the room. Claire hobbled over to the boxes and opened the first one. As she set things on the table, her gaze went about the room and stopped directly across from her.

"What is that?" She asked herself. Putting the bottle of solution on the table, she walked around it and headed for the far wall. She gasped as she recognized the dumbwaiter. She slid its door open and peered inside the huge compartment, wondering if it even worked anymore. She pushed the button to the right of the miniature elevator and jumped a bit as it began moving up, slamming her palm against the button again to bring it back down. Biting her lip as an idea formed in her mind, she turned and sat on the edge and then slid herself in backwards. Claire bit her lip at the throb in her hips and pulled herself in the rest of the way. Being very curious as to how far up it went, Claire reached over and hit the button, wrapping her arms around her knees as the dumbwaiter began its slow journey upwards.

She counted the doors on her way and held her breath as she passed the first door, wondering if anyone in the house could hear her. It ran remarkably silent for not being used in many years, and Claire giggled like a schoolgirl as she passed another door. She felt a bit surprised when it didn't stop at the third door, before realizing that the dumbwaiter must go all the way to the attic. She couldn't believe her luck at being able to get throughout the house without having to endure the pain of using the stairs. Claire silently clapped her hands together in excitement, totally anxious to see what she would find in the attic.

When her little personal elevator stopped, she slid the door open and gazed out into the dark attic. Frowning, she leaned out a bit to look for windows. She slid out of the dumbwaiter and limped her way over to the far wall. Light filtered around the edges of something propped on a few boxes. She focused on the large picture frame and moved it aside. The sudden brightness nearly blinded Claire, who shielded her eyes with her hand, before turning her back to the small round window.

Her gaze scanned the many boxes and articles that cluttered the large attic. As she looked around, she figured that the attic must cover the entire top of the house. She spotted the descending staircase on her right but paid it no mind, knowing that she would be going down the way she had come up. Claire looked from one item to the next: an old rocking horse, jack in the box, dollhouse, dolls, baby carriage, and the list went on and on. There had to be at least fifty boxes, all varying in size.

"Maybe that's why they're renting and not selling. They don't want to clean out this place," she said aloud with a smile. Claire looked back at the picture frame she had moved out of the way. It now leaned against the boxes beside her, and she reached for it. It had to be at least three feet high and maybe two feet wide. She immediately noticed the antique frame and absently wondered about its worth. As she remembered that nothing in the attic belonged to her, she shook her head at her own thought. Claire held the portrait up in front of her and gasped.

The woman within the frame certainly looked younger than Claire and far prettier. She had only seen the old fashioned hairdo in a few movies, as well as the style of her dark blue dress. Claire finally looked at the woman's face, and her eyes widened. She looked sort of lost and a bit sad. As she looked into the younger woman's eyes, she had the deepest desire to touch them. They seemed so real that it looked like a living photograph. That's what she thought at first, though as Claire held the frame closer to the light, she could clearly see the brush strokes. She reluctantly tore her gaze from those haunted eyes and looked at the bottom of the painting for the artist's name. She couldn't decipher the tiny scrawl and shook her head.

"So very beautiful," she sighed. Not wanting to leave the portrait in a dusty attic, Claire took it with her back to the dumbwaiter. Though she still wanted to explore, she might be missed soon and didn't want anyone to worry about her. The painting fit nicely in the back of the dumbwaiter, and Claire slid in beside it. The two of them then made their way back down to the basement.

Chapter 2

Claire pulled the painting out of the dumbwaiter and placed it on a stool against the wall. She stared at the woman, wishing she knew her name. The eyes beckoned to her, and Claire bit her lower lip in thought. She reached out a hand toward such truly exceptional work and wouldn't be surprised if the cheek were as smooth as it looked. When she heard the basement door open, she jumped back a step, grabbing the wall for support.

"Claire, honey, are you hungry? I've made us all some lunch." Her mother called down to her.

Claire sighed, thankful she had decided to come down from the attic when she did. "Thanks, Mom, I'll be right up."

"Do you need help, sweetie?"

Claire smiled and shook her head. "No thanks, Mom. I can make it on my own." She listened for the door closing and then turned back to the portrait. She stared at the woman's face again. "I'm going to find out who you are," she whispered before turning away and walking toward the staircase.

Claire's mind wandered as she ate her lunch. No one seemed to notice her distraction as the nonstop chatter filled the dining room. She didn't have a table yet, so everyone but Claire used the boxes or sat on the floor. Of course, no one minded that Claire sat in her desk chair and didn't take part in the discussion.

"Did you see that backyard? It's huge!"

"You should check out the third floor."

"I swear no one has lived here in decades."

She finally became aware that everyone stared at her. Her gaze went from one face to the other. "Yes?"

"We're just wondering why you wanted to rent such a huge place?" Her brother asked again.

Claire looked at Frank before giving them all a wistful smile and a shrug. "It just sort of called to me."

Her comment made her think of the woman's portrait downstairs. Had that been what called her and not necessarily the house? Something about the woman's eyes haunted her, so that she couldn't stop thinking about her. How long had the painting been sitting uncovered in that attic? It amazed her that it hadn't faded or been covered in cobwebs. It seemed as if even the spiders didn't want to touch it.

"How will you manage here all alone, Claire?" Emily asked softly.

She smiled at her sister. "I'll be just fine. I've wanted to live on my own for a while now. I think I'll be happy here." She paused to look at their concerned faces, "and it isn't as if you all live so far away. Mom and Dad are only a few miles from here." They nodded slowly.

Stefanie, her best friend, held up her glass, "and I'll come over often to help out, you know that!" She looked at the others. "I think we should toast to Claire's new adventure. Moving out on your own is a big deal!"

Everyone held up his or her glass. Claire held hers up last. "Here's to moving on." She added with a grin.

Once they had her settled in and thought the place livable, they all filed out of the house. Her mother gave her a tight hug, making sure to say one last time that she and her father were there if she needed them.

"I know, Mom! I'll be fine. Really, I will!"

She gave her Dad and siblings all a hug. Stefanie held back and waited to be the last to go.

"Do you want me to stick around a bit? We can rent a few movies and make some popcorn," she suggested.

As much as Claire liked spending time with her friend, she wanted to be alone in her new home. "That sounds great, but can I take a rain check? I really wanted to do some work tonight. I can't wait to try out my new dark room."

"Not a problem. Just call if you change your mind." Stefanie gave her a quick hug and then left.

Finally alone, Claire turned full circle, looking from the foyer to the living room, the staircase and then the sitting room. She could almost imagine how beautiful the house looked when it had been new. How unfortunate the owners had let it go so badly. Claire grabbed her purse, pulled out the realtor's business card, and dialed the number on her cell phone.

"Sam here," came the usual greeting.

"Hi, Sam, it's Claire Todds, I'm renting the house on Elm?"

"Ah, yes, what can I do for you, Ms. Todds?"

"Please, call me Claire. I wanted to know if you had any information on the people who own this house."

"Can I ask why, Claire?"

She shrugged, feeling her legs begin to stiffen. She walked over to her chair and sat down. "I was just wondering about all the boxes and things up in the attic?"

A brief pause greeted her question, before Sam cleared his throat. "You've been in the attic? You actually found the door?"

"Found it?" She sucked in her breath and closed her eyes. "er…was it supposed to be hidden?" She certainly didn't want to tell him that a grown woman had been using the dumbwaiter.

"Hmm…I guess not…well, that's why the house is not for sale. The Pruitts own it. Well, they both did until Mr. Pruitt died quite a number of years ago, and Mrs. Pruitt is now in a nursing home. She hasn't lived in that house for a long time but doesn't seem to want to part with it."

Claire frowned. "Do you know why?"

Sam paused and took a deep breath. "All I know is that they had a daughter who died, and the house is all they have left to remind them of her."

"A daughter?" Claire nearly gasped. "Do you know her name?"

"I never thought to pry…but why are you so interested, Claire?"

She sighed. "I guess being in their house, I feel a connection and want to know more about them."

"Then I'm sorry I can't be of more help. Mrs. Pruitt most likely doesn't have much longer to live…she's well over a hundred…and she didn't have any other children. I personally can't believe she's held on as long as she has...it's almost as if she's waiting for something...though I have no idea what that could be. Once she's gone, her family name dies with her."

Claire's hand went to her mouth. "That's so sad." She swallowed the lump in her throat. "Why has she decided to rent…after all this time?"

Sam chuckled. "I asked her that very thing."

"And?" Claire prodded, sensing he didn't want to tell her.

"Well, it's silly, but what the hell? Mrs. Pruitt said she dreamt of her daughter, who asked her to."

"Her daughter asked her to rent the house?"

"That's what she said." He chuckled again. "Maybe you'll meet her someday to hear the whole story. She's really a sweet old thing."

"I'd like that."

"Well, was there anything else I can help you with, Ms. Todds…I mean, Claire?"

She smiled. "No, Sam, that's it. Thanks, though. You've been a lot of help." She opened her mouth to say bye, when something occurred to her. "Oh, one last thing. Why didn't you tell me the attic was off limits when I rented the place? I mean, don't I have the right to access everything here?"

She could hear him sigh before responding. "Ordinarily, I would say yes…but honestly, I never thought you'd even find the attic, let alone realize there was one. That staircase is quite hidden. I'm actually surprised you found it."

Claire repeated his words to herself, *the staircase is quite hidden*. "Well, I guess I can understand why they wouldn't want anyone going up there. There's a lot of stuff. You don't have to tell Mrs. Pruitt that I was up there. I won't damage anything."

"I'm sure you won't. Well, be sure to let me know if you need anything else, Claire."

"OK, thanks again, Sam."

She turned off her cell phone and stared around the room. Groaning as she pushed herself off the chair, she walked over to the fireplace and let her gaze travel above the mantel. Claire noticed the hook high up on the wall. She reached over to turn on the nearest lamp and immediately noticed the rectangular section of dark wallpaper. A picture had obviously hung there for quite some time. Claire took a step closer and tried to judge the size. She nodded as she realized that it looked roughly three feet high and two feet wide, the perfect fit of the portrait she found in the attic.

Claire knew she should do some work in the dark room. She had a few rolls of film that needed developing, but her curiosity got the better of her. She had to find that hidden staircase to the attic. Not wanting to go down to the basement to get to the dumbwaiter, Claire walked to the back of the house in search of it on the first floor. She walked past it several times before she finally saw it. The camouflaged door resembled the rest of the wall. She slid it open and then stuck her head in. Of course, the little elevator still sat in the basement, so she pushed the button to have it ascend to her level. Claire smiled as she made another journey up through the house. Had Sam not thought of her using the dumbwaiter, because he didn't know it existed? She knew about it and still had trouble finding it. Claire fully expected it to be similarly camouflaged on the other two floors.

She arrived on the third floor and pulled herself out of the dumbwaiter. She closed the door behind her and stepped back, not at all disappointed. She nodded as the door blended with the rest of the wall. "That's incredible," she muttered to herself.

Claire finally turned away from the wall and looked around the third floor. She tried to visualize the attic and where she had seen the staircase, and then she walked in that direction. Two large bedrooms were in that area, so Claire went from one room to the other and then back again.

"It has to be here somewhere," she said with a bit of frustration. Her hips were beginning to ache, and she hadn't brought her cane with her. Needing to sit down for a moment, she stepped back and sat on the bed. She suddenly focused on the furniture and looked around in surprise. There had been none on the first floor, so she was quite surprised to see the room completely furnished. As she stared at the canopy above her head and the dolls on the shelves, she realized this must be the bedroom of the Pruitts' daughter. Claire's gaze went from the China dolls to the writing desk and then to the full-length antique mirror in the corner. She saw her own dusty reflection staring back.

Pushing herself off the bed and approaching the writing desk, she slid the cover open. Claire sat at the desk and just stared at first, almost afraid to disturb anything. She looked from the fountain pens to the stack of paper tied with some string. Deciding that she had to see if the girl kept a journal or diary, Claire began to look through the drawers. About to give up, Claire felt the bottom of one of the drawers shift. Realizing she might have found a secret compartment, Claire pried the wood loose and revealed a diary.

"Yes!" She yelled triumphantly, pulling the book free from the compartment. She opened the cover and read the inscription on the first page.

Faith M Pruitt ~ 1926 –

No ending year had been written. Claire figured that Faith must have forgotten about her diary as she grew up. She flipped to the last page with anything written on it, which had the date of August 29th, 1935. She then flipped to the front, hoping that Faith would have mentioned how old she had been in 1926. Claire smiled as she read the first entry, obviously written by a child. The short entry was dated April 18th.

Dear Diary,

Hello! Mummy got you for me on my birthday. I am eight years old today. She told me to write all my secrets in here for you alone, but I have no secrets.

Faith

Claire couldn't hold back the chuckle as she flipped back to the last entry.

Dear Diary,

I am sad today. There doesn't seem to be any way I can get out of this marriage. Mum says that I am at a marriageable age. She doesn't care that I do not love Hank. She says that will come in time. Just between us, I do not see that happening in my lifetime. Wish me luck! I will need it.

Yours, Faith

As she read Faith's last words in her diary, the smile left her face. Not wanting to read anymore, Claire closed the book and put it on the desk. She did the math in her head and realized that Faith had been only seventeen when she wrote that last entry. Mrs. Pruitt forced her only child to marry a man that she did not like, and she was only seventeen. Claire just couldn't wrap her mind around it. At least she now knew why the woman didn't want to sell the house. After Faith died, the guilt must nearly have consumed her.

Claire looked around the room, suddenly remembering her primary purpose for being there. She still hadn't found the hidden staircase. Inspiration struck as she stood and walked over to the walk-in closet. She went from one side to the other, tapping lightly, until she came across a hollow sound. Realizing she had stumbled upon another camouflaged door, she worked at it until she got it open. As she revealed the staircase, Claire smiled.

"There you are." She stood back and stared at it, vaguely wondering if the house had many other hidden doors. She couldn't hold back the smile as she anticipated finding them.

Chapter 3

Claire sat in a booth with Stefanie about to order their dinners. Claire looked over the menu with a distracted gaze. Her friend noticed and put her hand on the top of the menu, pushing it down slightly. Claire looked up with a puzzled expression.

"You seem so distracted. Are you alright, Claire?" Stefanie asked with a soft smile.

Claire shrugged, letting the menu drop to the table. She really didn't have an appetite and hadn't even wanted to go out. She just knew that her friend wanted to spend time with her. Normally she enjoyed going out with Stefanie, but Claire wanted to be in her new home. It had been two days since she moved in and hadn't had much time to search for more hidden doors. The editor of the magazine called to remind her of the deadline for her expected photos. She had been postponing everything because of the move, and she knew she couldn't keep putting it off. She had even been on her way to her dark room, when Stefanie phoned. Realizing that she needed to do some work first, she postponed their dinner to give her more time to develop all the photos and get them sent off to the magazine.

She sighed. "I've just been really busy with work...and the house is still a mess."

Stefanie chuckled. "It will always be a mess. I can't help but wonder why you wanted to rent it in the first place."

Claire stared off into space for a moment before shrugging again. "I can't explain what I'm not even completely sure about."

"You just need to get out more often. How about letting me fix you up again? Brad has the nicest new friend, and he's such a cutie!"

Claire began to shake her head halfway through Stefanie's appeal, and her friend frowned.

"You don't want to be alone forever, do you? It just kills me to think of you in that big house all by yourself. You have *so* much to offer someone, Claire. I just wish you could see that, too."

Claire met her friend's sad gaze for a moment before smiling. "Do you know what I've always felt about fate?" She waited for Stefanie to shake her head. "We are all supposed to believe that everyone has a soul mate that we're destined to meet and be happy with, right? But what happens if your soul mate is killed before you ever have the chance to meet them… or if for some reason they never even have the chance to be born? What then?" She sighed and dropped her chin into the palm of her hand. "Have you lost your one chance at happiness? Well, that's how I feel sometimes. I really don't believe that there is a Mr. Right for me out there, let alone one that will accept me the way I am."

"The way you are, Claire? Why, because of that accident? So what if you walk a little funny.

That doesn't take away from how beautiful you are. You must know that?" Stefanie responded passionately, almost near tears.

Claire didn't want to upset her friend. After all, she and Stefanie had been friends since high school. She had been there throughout the hospital stays and the rehabilitation that followed. Sometimes Claire didn't believe she would have made it without her friend. Not liking to see Stefanie upset, Claire nodded. "Of course, you're right. I'm just being a bit melodramatic…that's all!"

Stefanie still frowned. "You sure? Well, all I can say is that I wish that old bastard had hit me instead. After all, I was the gymnast. I would surely have rolled out of the way."

The comment hit Claire so strangely that she burst out laughing. "Now where on Earth did you ever get such an idea?" She asked through the laughter, tears brimming her eyes.

Stefanie joined in the laughter. "I just wish they had checked his vision regularly…God, how old *was* he anyway? 86? Now that is just way too old to be driving."

Claire stopped laughing. "Well, he's surely got to be dead by now, wouldn't you think?" As she asked it, she remembered that Mrs. Pruitt was still alive at over a hundred. She vaguely wondered how much longer the old woman would live. Maybe she would do a bit of research to find out if that old man still lived. She wondered if he ever thought about her and how he had forever changed her life. She couldn't even recall his name, though it would most likely be in the newspaper article. At that moment Claire decided she would do some research as soon as she got home!

She sighed deeply, giving Stefanie a bright smile. "Let's just enjoy our dinner, shall we?"

Her friend nodded her head and wiped her eyes. "Yes, let's!"

Claire limped into her house a few hours later. She regretted not taking the cane with her but hated using it in public. Her hips ached and tears began to fill her eyes. She let Stefanie talk her into a movie after dinner, and everything stiffened up during the show. She hadn't wanted to ruin the evening for her friend, so she dealt with the discomfort as best she could.

Claire held the wall as she moved toward the nearest chair, tears of frustration and pain finally spilling down her cheeks. Luckily, she didn't have to endure such days that often, or her life would be sheer hell. She landed heavily on the chair and began to massage her hips and thighs. At that moment she hated her life. She would never understand the injustice of being run down as a teenager and having to feel like an old arthritic woman for the rest of her life. "I'm only twenty-six, for Christ sake!" She yelled to the empty room. "It's not fair!" She pounded her fists against her thighs and leaned forward on the chair, letting her hair hang over her knees.

As she cried and felt sorry for herself, her thoughts shifted to Faith Pruitt. Claire thought about the injustice of being forced to marry a man she didn't like and not being able to stop it. As she thought of that poor seventeen year-old girl, her tears began to dry on her cheeks. Claire had been only a year younger than that when she lost the full use of her legs.

Wiping the remaining tears from her eyes, Claire forced herself to her feet and walked to the back of the house. She opened the door to the dumbwaiter and crawled inside, pushing the down button. When it stopped at the basement, she reached out and grabbed hold of the portrait frame to pull it into the dumbwaiter with her. Claire stared at the young face, somehow confident that she stared at Faith Pruitt. She then pushed the up button and got out at the first floor. Claire grunted through the pain and stiffness in her body, as she walked back into the living room.

She stared up at the hook on the wall and realized it was out of her reach. She took a deep breath and leaned the portrait against the wall on the mantel. She sighed through her clenched teeth, as she pulled the chair closer to the wall and climbed on top of it. Claire closed her eyes as a jolt of pain flew through her hip, and she hung on to the mantel for support. She rested her forehead against the cool wall and waited for the pain to subside. When it had, she grabbed hold of the frame on either side and lifted it.

She knew that she wouldn't be able to stay on the chair for long and could only hope the frame caught on her first attempt. Claire let out a gasp of surprise when it did. She nearly fell off the chair but grabbed hold of the mantel again, slowly easing herself to the floor.

Claire stepped back and looked up at Faith's portrait with a smile. "Welcome home, Faith," she whispered softly. "I have some research to do now."

Clair sat on her bed and looked through a box beside her. She sifted through old pictures and photo albums until she found what she sought. She set the open album on her lap and gazed at the newspaper clipping.

"Damn, Stefanie, you have a better memory than I do," she muttered to herself as she scanned the article. "Holmes, 86, proclaims he didn't see the teenager run out in front of his car." She read with a shake of her head. "I didn't run, you jerk, and I was in the crosswalk." Claire looked at the photo of the old man and had a hard time meeting his gaze. Something about his eyes was a bit off. She barely remembered him after the accident, but she knew she'd met him once. She then looked at her own photo in the clipping. They had used her current high school yearbook photo. She had been so young then. Claire had a hard time believing it had only been ten years, since it felt so much longer.

She shoved the albums and photos back into the box before walking over to her desk and turning on her computer. Since Stefanie had mentioned it, Claire needed to know if the old codger were still alive. She logged onto the Internet and searched the national archives. Didn't take long to find his obituary, and she read the article. Claire frowned to see that he had no surviving family members, not even children. When she read the date, her eyes widened. He had died the year after his car struck her. She closed her eyes from the irony of it and shook her head. Claire sighed and read the rest of the article. He had been born, raised and died in the same city, which surprised her. She would have thought to remain in his hometown his whole life that he would have family around. Deciding to do a bit more research on him, she dug a bit deeper. Claire had always been good at doing research or really anything on the computer. Not being able to run around with friends or take part in sports left a lot of free time on her hands.

Unfortunately, Mr. Holmes hadn't done much to be recognized for during his long life, other than dying a wealthy widower. His last wife had made the paper by doing charity work, and she was mentioned as his fifth wife.

"Five wives, huh?" Claire commented and continued her searching, but she gave up an hour later. He had managed to stay under the radar most of his life, and she couldn't even find announcements for his other weddings.

Deciding she had wasted enough time on him, she switched the theme of her searching to Faith. After half an hour, she realized the futility of trying to find anything on the woman. The only thing she could find was the obituary for Mr. Pruitt. She doubted anyone had even scanned most of the old papers onto the Internet, which was the problem of living in such a small town. Claire bit her lip as she contemplated the worth of going to the public library and actually searching through the archives on microfilm.

As she realized she needed to find out what happened to Faith Pruitt, she nodded and pushed away from her computer. She stood too quickly, and her hip gave out. Claire crashed to the floor with a scream of pain. She had clearly pushed herself too far and would have to postpone any trip to the library. Claire drug herself across the room and reached for her purse, pulling it to the floor with her. She dug through it until she found her pain pills, popped the top and shook out three of them. As she rolled onto her back, she dropped them all in her mouth and swallowed them without water. Claire stared up at the ceiling, tears sliding down her face, and waited for the merciful numbness to claim her.

When Claire awoke, she could barely open her eyes to focus. She felt hung over and pushed herself to a seated position. Her whole body felt numb, but she cringed out of habit. Yawning, she grabbed hold of the bed beside her and pulled herself up to her knees and then her feet. Claire sighed as she looked at the clock beside the bed to discover it was just past three in the morning. She shook her head to clear it and blinked her eyes a few times. Not wanting to wear herself out again, she grabbed the cane leaning against the wall and used it to stand. Claire hobbled out to the living room and stared up at Faith's haunted face.

"I wish you could tell me what happened to you."

As the woman in the portrait stared back, a light bulb went off in Claire's head. She had kept a clipping of her terrible accident, so maybe Faith's parents kept newspaper clippings of their only daughter. Claire bit her lip in thought. Would they want to keep the memory of her death? She shrugged and then nodded. People were generally morbid that way, but where would they keep something like that? Claire looked toward the ceiling, as if seeing the attic through the levels above her. She then walked into the kitchen to fetch a flashlight before heading to the dumbwaiter.

After an hour Claire began to lose confidence of ever finding anything useful. The battery in her flashlight grew dim, and she had already gone through about a dozen boxes. Most of them had clothing or dishes or knick-knacks inside. Maybe the Pruitts had taken their photo albums with them, which did make the most sense. Claire sighed, about to give up, when she opened another box and gasped.

"Jackpot," she breathed with relief. She adjusted herself on the box she sat upon and reached into the open box in front of her, pulling out a stack of photo albums. She shined the light on the front of each of them, thankful that they had all been dated. When she got to the one dated "1933 to", she froze. All the others had a range of years on them…all of them but this one. Claire looked into the now empty box and frowned, realizing there must not have any other albums after the 1930's. A shiver ran down her back, as she took a deep breath and opened the album.

Claire gasped as she saw the first black and white photo of Faith. Her name had been written beneath the aged photo, so Claire finally knew for sure who had sat for that portrait. Tears filled her eyes as she looked at the pretty young teenager. She didn't even have to guess her age, since 15 was written beside her name. The captioned photos made it easy for Claire to discover everyone's names. There were photos of both Mr. and Mrs. Pruitt, whose names turned out to be Hector and Margie. Faith seemed to be a happy girl, who smiled in every picture. The haunted look in the portrait came to Claire's mind. She certainly hadn't been smiling when that had been painted.

Claire flipped through the years until she reached the summer of 1935. The smiling girl went away, and the sulky young woman replaced her. Claire frowned upon seeing the first picture of Hank and held the album closer to her face to get a better look. She groaned as she moved the flashlight closer, but the grainy picture and dim light made it hard to see him clearly. Claire sighed and flipped another page. She smiled at seeing her first newspaper clipping. It announced Faith's upcoming marriage to Hank. She scanned it looking for a date. The announcement had been published on

August 15th, 1935. Claire frowned, trying to remember that last date in Faith's diary. It eluded her at first and then jumped into her mind. It had been August 29th, almost two weeks after the announcement. She looked again at the article to find the date of the wedding, but it only stated, "to be announced later." Claire sighed and flipped another page. She held her breath and then let it out slowly. She had expected more pictures before the wedding, so she stared in surprise at an 8" by 10" photo of the wedding party.

"Oh, my!" Claire sighed and looked from one face to the next. Her gaze stopped on Faith's miserable face, before moving to Hank's leer. Claire shook her head at such an expression, instantly disliking the man and immediately looked at the next face. She stopped again with a gasp, her gaze temporarily dropping to the caption beneath the photo. She read the names and stopped on his: Hector, Margie, Faith, Hank, Janet and Noah. Claire whispered his name as her gaze returned to his face.

"Noah," she sighed, and a chill ran through her. It took her a moment before she remembered she wanted to know the date of the wedding. She looked at the clipping on the facing page. "September 7th?" She asked out loud. Claire shook her head in bewilderment as her gaze returned to Noah's face. She didn't even realize a smile spread across her lips, and she moved a hand closer. As she realized she was about to caress the photo, she pulled her hand back. Claire chuckled to herself and rubbed her hands across her face. Noah had probably been dead for many years. Instead of that making her feel better, she felt hollow inside and a bit sad. She had the feeling that she would have liked the man. He had such a gentle and open face. She looked at him one last time before she flipped the page. What she saw next made her gasp in shock. The album slid off her lap and landed on the floor with a thud. It remained opened though, and Claire slowly leaned forward to peer down at it. As she read the date and the headline, she shook her head in denial.

"No," she moaned and read the headline again. *Newlywed and Best Man die in tragic boating mishap.* Tears filled her eyes as she reached down to pick up the album, but she couldn't look away from the date. Faith Pruitt had died September 10th, 1935, only three days after her wedding.

Chapter 4

Claire immersed herself in work to try to get her mind off the old newspaper clipping, but she failed miserably. Even as she rinsed and hung her new photos, her mind kept seeing that headline. She had read the article, at least most of it, since the shock of it all made concentrating difficult. It seemed that instead of going on a honeymoon on their own, Hank and Faith had gone on a shared holiday with the entire family, including their best man and maid of honor. Claire figured the newly-weds didn't know each other very well, and that it might be easier for their family and friends to be with them to help out. They all had vacationed at a posh lake resort. None of them had ever been on a yacht apparently, and an afternoon excursion on the lake had ended two of their lives.

According to the article, Hank had taken his new bride and his best friend out on the lake. Janet, the maid of honor, hadn't been included for some unmentioned reason. Remembering how she had felt when she looked at the picture of Hank, Claire's lip curled as a reason sprang to mind. Janet either didn't like Hank, or she hadn't been invited.

When the yacht docked later in the day, only Hank was aboard. He ran into the resort, drenched and shouting like a madman. He told everyone that things had gone horribly wrong and that both his bride and friend had fallen into the lake. He had gone in after them but hadn't been able to find them. The authorities had been called and search parties had been sent out on the lake. While they were out, the police had questioned Hank. Being the only survivor, they only had his version to go by.

According to Hank the three of them had a wonderful time until the wind changed. Hank thought he knew more than he did about sailing and asked Noah to help with the rigging. During a wind shift, the sail struck Noah and knocked him overboard. Hank told officials that he had immediately dove in after his friend and spent countless minutes trying to find him. He sadly reported that after being forced to give up and return to the yacht, he couldn't find Faith. Not knowing what else to do, he turned the boat around and headed for the dock.

It took a few hours before they found the bodies. Both had bruises on their heads and had drowned, so the authorities concluded that the sail had hit both Noah and Faith and knocked them overboard. Hank was appropriately mournful when informed, and the authorities ruled the deaths as accidental.

"Yeah, right!" Claire yelled to the dark basement. She stared at the photo she had just developed but didn't see it. Tears clouded her eyes, and she shook her head. She didn't even know why she cared so much about people that had died years before her own birth. They had been dead before Claire's own mother had been born.

She might still need to go to the library and do some research on Hank. Claire realized she had to find out what became of him. Something about him troubled her, and she'd like to get to the bottom of her feelings about him. She felt certain that he had killed Faith and Noah. She nearly choked as she thought about him. Claire didn't even like to think about the fact that Noah had died as well. She had felt such a connection to him, and it depressed her to discover he died so tragically. She felt very near tears again. To mourn two people that she had never met seemed silly, but she couldn't help it. She felt connected to them somehow. Like she should have been able to stop their murders. Yes, that's what she called it. She knew in her gut that Hank had murdered them both.

Claire couldn't sleep that night. Bad dreams plagued her every time she closed her eyes. She saw Hank with a shovel. He came up behind Faith and struck her in the back of the head. She heard a gasp and saw Noah. He had witnessed Hank trying to kill his wife. He came to her aide, and Hank turned on his friend. He attacked Noah with the shovel, hitting him in the forehead with it. Hank looked indecisive for a moment but then carried their unconscious bodies to the yacht. He sailed out to the middle of the lake and then dropped them into the water. He watched with an evil grin as they sank to the bottom.

She sat up with a scream. Claire clutched the covers and looked around at the shadows in her room. "No!" She yelled to the heavens. Had her own feelings for Hank created that dream or was it the truth? How would she know what had happened that many years ago?

Claire threw back the covers and swung her legs over the edge of the bed. She cringed but forced herself to ignore the pain in her hips. She pushed herself off the mattress, holding onto the wall for support. Claire bit her upper lip as she steadied herself and then took a few steps away from the bed. Her legs were always the most uncooperative when she first woke up, but she concentrated on each step and soon found herself standing beneath Faith's portrait. Claire looked up at it and shook her head.

"What do you want from me?" She asked in a small voice. "I can't help you. I wish I could." She swallowed the lump in her throat. "I wish I could help you both." Tears filled her eyes as she thought of all the sorrow associated with that painting. Claire suddenly realized that it didn't need to be hanging in her living room. She would never have any peace if she kept thinking about it or looking at it. Tears streamed down her cheeks as she grabbed a poker from the fireplace and pushed it against the bottom of the frame. It lifted off the hook and then slid down the wall, landing with a thud on the mantel. Claire gasped as it started to fall toward her, and she held up her hands to catch it. Her eyes widened as she came face to face with Faith. She sank to the floor, never breaking eye contact with the troubled teenager. "I'm so sorry, Faith. I wish I could help you," she sobbed, her hand moving toward the painted cheek. As her palm touched the canvas, warmth flew up her arm and spread throughout her body. Claire tried to jump back, but she felt herself being sucked in...into the painting. She tried to scream but then all went black.

Chapter 5

Claire moaned as she rolled over. She felt sick to her stomach and feared opening her eyes, afraid to see the room spinning. She moved a hand to her head and rubbed her temple. After swallowing a few times, Claire willed herself not to get sick. The last thing she needed was to throw up on herself, since she couldn't get to the bathroom in time. She sat up with a groan and rubbed her other temple, taking a few deep breaths.

Slowly opening her eyes and focusing on her surroundings, Claire looked around in puzzlement. As she recognized Faith's room, she wondered how she had gotten there from the living room on the first floor. She then took a closer look at the room and noticed how everything looked shiny and new. Claire stood and walked over to the shelf of new dolls. The last time she saw them, the dresses were aged, faded and dusty.

Claire shook her head, wondering if it could be a dream. She nodded, deciding that must be it. She chuckled and sat on the edge of the bed. At that moment she spotted the full-length mirror across the room. The lack of dust didn't surprise her as much as her reflection shocked her.

"Oh, my God!" She breathed softly and stood to approach the mirror. Faith's reflection also approached, and their hands met on the surface of the glass. Claire jumped back with a squeak, only then realizing that her hips and legs didn't hurt. "If this is a dream, it sure is a vivid one," she said aloud, spinning around and then jumping in place. "Nothing hurts!" She shouted with a laugh.

She sucked in her breath as she heard someone running up the stairs. An older woman rushed into the room, causing Claire to look around for a place to hide.

"What's all the shouting about? Are you alright, Faith?"

On the verge of breaking out in a case of nervous giggles, Claire recognized the woman from the photo album as Faith's mother, Margie.

"Uh…yes, mother, I'm fine." She had to bite her tongue to keep from smiling, but Margie frowned at her.

"What's so funny? What have you been doing up here? Dinner is almost ready, and you don't want to keep your betrothed waiting. He's been downstairs for over ten minutes already."

Claire's eyes widened, all mirth leaving her instantly. "Hank's here?" She asked breathlessly.

"Of course, he's here." Margie approached her and placed a hand to her forehead. "You're not becoming ill, are you?"

"No, I feel fine." She responded, stepping back. Claire licked her lips, for the first time wondering if maybe this wasn't a dream after all. "I'll be right down."

"Be quick about it, young lady," Faith's mother admonished as she left the room and went back downstairs.

Claire nearly collapsed into the desk chair. She tapped her fingers on the desk and then remembered the diary. She pulled it out of the secret compartment and flipped it to the last entry. "Oh, no," she muttered as she read the same August 29th entry. Was it presently the 29th or had Faith written that the day before or even earlier? Claire had to find out the date. She had to know how much time she had before the wedding. Claire bit her lip as she put the diary back into its hiding place. She took a deep breath and stood, running her hands down the front of her skirt. She frowned and looked down at what she wore. She moved to stand before the mirror again and shook her head at the style of dress in the 1930's. "I guess it could be worse," she joked. "I could have been sent back to the 20's." She nearly laughed at the idea of being dressed as a flapper with one of those horrible short haircuts. At least Faith had long hair, though she had it twisted and curled into a strange style.

"Damn, I look like Joan Crawford from *Mommie Dearest*." Claire slapped a hand over her mouth as giggles threatened to overcome her again. As she fought to control them, she hoped she wasn't going crazy. She shook her head and cleared her throat, before turning toward the door. She was about to meet the man that married and murdered Faith. She blinked a few times and then left the bedroom.

Claire stopped outside the sitting room. She looked around and smiled at the grandeur of the house. She knew it had once been very beautiful. Claire licked her dry lips as she listened to the conversation going on in the sitting room.

"Yes, sir, I agree that Popeye is a funny and entertaining cartoon."

"Well, I personally prefer Betty Boop. I just love her voice."

Claire frowned as she heard the young voices. Who else could be in that sitting room besides Faith's parents? Knowing of only one way to find out, she stepped over the threshold. No one noticed her at first, and she took a good look at Hank. She had to admit to his good looks, but he no doubt put on a good show for the parents. Claire swallowed another lump in her throat as she looked from Margie to Hector, Faith's father, and then a girl about Faith's age. She smiled as she recognized Janet, the maid of honor, who must be Faith's best friend. As if sensing the stare, Janet turned her head and noticed Faith in the doorway. Her face lit up, and she gestured to her.

"You're finally here," she announced, bringing all eyes to Faith.

Claire tried not to groan and forced a smile, as she entered the room. The men stood as she neared. Janet met her half way, taking her hand and tugging her along the rest of the way. Claire felt an immediate fondness for the girl, thankful that nothing bad became of her. Knowing she would eventually have to make eye contact with Hank, Claire mustered up her courage and looked up at him. She flinched as she stared into his depthless eyes. She had never seen such eyes and couldn't keep looking at them, instead focusing on his mouth. His smile would have looked genuine if she hadn't seen his eyes first. A shiver went down her spine as he took her hand.

"It's so good to see you again, Faith. I've counted the minutes since our last visit."

Claire tried not to gag and held her other hand up to her mouth to hide her expression. "Yes, well, that's nice." She was about to pull her hand free, when a voice from the door interrupted.

"Sorry, I'm late all! Have I missed any of the wedding talk?"

Claire sucked in her breath as Noah rushed into the room. Her jaw dropped as she watched him shake hands with Hector and then Hank, which gave her a good reason to pull free of his clutches. Her breathing grew shallow to be face to face with the man and not just his photo. Where Hank had dark hair and eyes, Noah's fair hair and blue eyes gave him the face of an angel. She couldn't believe how his very presence sent butterflies erupting within her stomach. Claire crossed her arms over herself, as if everyone in the room could see them. She heard nothing but buzzing as they all welcomed Noah. He finally looked at her with a warm smile, and she thought she would melt into the floor.

"And how are you this fine evening, Miss Faith?"

She opened her mouth but nothing came out.

"Well, speak up, girl. Don't be rude," Faith's father barked.

She flinched at his tone, sparing him a quick glance before nodding. "Just fine, Noah, and you?" Her lower lip quivered as she said his name.

"Now that my best man has finally arrived, I guess we can get to dinner?" Hank said, clapping an arm around Noah's shoulders. Claire's gaze went from Noah to Hank and then returned to Noah. How could two such opposite men be friends?

Claire floated in a fog for the rest of the evening. She knew they discussed her future, or at least the future they thought Faith had, but she couldn't concentrate on what they said. Every once in a while, she snuck glances at Noah. A few times he would be staring at her, and she would quickly look away. His adorable smile forced her to bite her lip to keep from returning it. She only needed to look at Hank to wipe any remnants of a smile from her face. When he didn't think anyone looked his way, he very nearly scowled. Once he noticed Claire staring at him, a smile quickly replaced the scowl. She hated him at that moment and forced a smile. True, she loathed him before she met him, but she truly hated him right then. She would do everything in her power to stop the wedding. In fact she would make sure she never had to be alone with him at all.

After the meal, Janet pulled her aside. "Faith, are you alright? You were awfully quiet during dinner."

Claire shook her head. If this were truly her best friend, she must know how Faith felt about Hank. "I was just trying to think of a way to get out of this wedding."

Janet looked ready to cry at her words. "Short of running away? You know your parents will disown you if you break off this engagement."

Claire's eyes widened at the comment. "They would, huh?" She muttered under her breath. No wonder Faith married the bastard. She had been pressured into it. Claire smirked and shook her head. "Well, I won't be so easily pressured. I won't marry that man."

Janet smiled with glee and clasped hands with her. "I'm so happy to hear you say that."

Claire looked at their joined hands before refocusing on the girl's face. She couldn't understand Janet's enthusiasm at her refusal to get married. Deciding to ignore the thoughts that began to enter her mind, she smiled. "Me, too!"

They joined the others in the living room. Claire's gaze immediately sought out Noah, who stood near the fireplace. Claire involuntarily looked above the mantel, half expecting to see the painting. She sucked in her breath, surprised that she had forgotten about it until then.

"My painting!" She announced to the others. "Where is my painting?"

At first no one spoke, but then Faith's mother frowned at her. "You weren't even supposed to know about that. The artist is coming over in the morning to paint you! How on Earth did you find out? It was supposed to be a surprise." She turned to Hank with a forced chuckle. "It was to be a wedding present for you."

Hank's stare made Claire uncomfortable, and she shifted from one foot to the other. "How very lovely, Mrs. Pruitt. I will look forward to seeing it when it's done."

Claire looked again at the spot above the fireplace, where currently hung an abstract painting. Her gaze then dropped to Noah, who still leaned against the mantel. He gave her a soft smile, and this time she gave into her impulse and returned it.

Chapter 6

Claire didn't have to worry about being forced to be alone with Hank. Her parents thought it inappropriate for an unmarried couple to go anywhere without a chaperone, so either Janet or Noah always accompanied them. Claire still hadn't figured out the date, and there didn't seem to be calendars anywhere in the house. She didn't want to come out and ask the date, but the conversation did eventually get around to that discussion. Faith's parents retired to the sitting room a short while later, telling the young people to have an enjoyable evening together.

"Well, it's still early, folks. What do you kids want to do on this fine Friday night?" Noah asked with a grin, looking from Hank to Janet and then Claire, who lit up at finding out the day. She had to bite her lip to keep from asking if that meant it was the 30th. She hoped she wouldn't be unlucky enough for it to be the 6th, since the wedding took place the following day. A week would give her more time to formulate a plan of action.

"We always go to the movies on Friday," Janet said softly, looking nervously at Claire, who almost laughed. The very idea of watching a movie from 1935 had her nearly cringing.

"That sounds like a great idea. There's a double feature at the theater. I think it premiered last week. It's about a cowboy named *Hopalong Cassidy*. I've actually been looking forward to seeing it." Hank contributed, giving Claire a grin that looked more like a leer. "I just love westerns."

Claire swallowed the lump in her throat, almost revealing how much she hated westerns but instead smiled and nodded her head. "That sounds fine." Unfortunately, not being a 1935 movie buff she had no idea when *Hopalong Cassidy* premiered.

"Too bad *Top Hat* isn't starting tonight. I'm really looking forward to seeing that," Janet said with enthusiasm, smiling at Claire. "We'll be seeing that next Friday, right? Unless getting married the next day will interfere with our plans?" She added, trying to keep the smile in place.

Claire almost laughed again. So she did have a week until the wedding. "*Top Hat* is premiering on September 6th, which is a week away?" She clarified for herself, and Janet nodded. "No, that sounds fine with me." *Top H*at didn't ring any familiar bells either, but she felt relieved to know the wedding wouldn't take place the following day. "So, no bachelorette party planned, huh?" Claire asked before she could stop herself. She doubted any such thing existed in 1935, and judging by Janet's expression, it didn't.

"A what?" Janet asked.

Noah laughed. "Bachelorette party? How modern of you, Miss Pruitt. After all, that's what your future husband and I will be doing that night. Isn't that right, Hank?"

Hank gave Claire another disturbing look, before glancing at his friend. "Well, it's called a bachelor party, Noah."

"Oh, sorry, I meant a wedding shower?" She asked, still unsure of the proper 30's term. Janet's confusion melted away, and she giggled.

"You silly goose! That was last weekend."

Claire sighed. "Of course, it was! I was just teasing." She then realized she needed to read Faith's diary as soon as she got the time.

The four of them piled into Hank's car and headed for the theater. Claire sat in the front seat beside Hank, though she stayed as close to the door as she could. It had troubled her at first when she couldn't find the seat belt, but she managed to stop herself before asking about it. The car obviously didn't have them, so she nervously endured the entire ride.

Claire looked out the window as they drove along, totally captivated by what she saw. Even though they had finished dinner, the summer sun still shone. She looked at all the old fashioned cars and the people in their outdated clothing and smiled.

"So, you're having your portrait done tomorrow?" Hank's voice cut through the peaceful setting, and she turned to him sharply.

"I suppose I am," she slowly responded. "Do you like sailing, Hank?" She asked suddenly. "I meant does anyone here like sailing?" Claire looked in the back seat at Noah and Janet.

No one answered at first, so she continued. "Because I don't think I like it at all. In fact I don't think you could catch me dead on a yacht."

Janet's mouth fell open in surprise, but she didn't speak. Claire bit her lower lip to keep from smiling and looked at Noah. His brows lifted, and he looked a bit confused but clearly fought a smile.

Claire returned her gaze to Hank, whose face turned red. "You know I like to sail, Faith...and Noah does as well. We're both very accomplished on the water."

"Oh, really?" She asked in genuine surprise, looking at Noah for confirmation. He nodded slowly, clearly not understanding her strange comments. Claire turned back to Hank, wondering why that bit of information eluded the authorities. After all they had thought Noah's ineptness at sailing led to his death.

"Yes, really, and you know very well where we will be vacationing after the wedding. So now you say you don't want to go sailing?" Hank continued, clearly holding onto his temper.

Claire took a deep breath. "I guess I changed my mind. Isn't that a lady's prerogative?"

Hank glared at her for an instant before his polite mask slipped into place. "Of course, you can change your mind. I just don't know what's gotten into you." He looked in the rearview mirror. "Is it just me, Noah, or is she acting different than usual?"

Claire turned to look at Noah, her own brows rising and awaited his response. Noah gave her a quick grin before meeting Hank's gaze in the mirror. "Well, I do notice a bit of change, but I…I kind of like it."

Hank rolled his eyes with a low growl. "Yeah, but you don't have to marry her."

Claire shot daggers at the man before turning to look back at Noah with a smile, her look clearly stating she wished the opposite were true. Noah seemed to read her expression, and his eyes widened in surprise. Leaving him with that notion, she turned away and looked out the windshield.

"Neither do you," she said aloud, crossing her arms in front of her.

She could see that Hank turned to look at her, but he didn't respond. They then drove along in silence.

When they arrived at the theater, Janet pulled Claire aside and told the men they needed to use the ladies room. Janet very nearly drug Claire inside.

"What's going on, Faith?" Janet asked, clearly hurt and confused.

"What do you mean?" She asked.

"You aren't acting like yourself. I mean, I don't care what that man said, but I'm noticing it myself. You're not even talking like yourself…and what is going on with you and Noah?" She shook her head, her eyes brimming with tears.

"What do you mean?" Claire repeated.

"You keep smiling at him and staring at him. Don't think I haven't noticed. You tell me that you won't marry Hank. Now I'm wondering if that's for me…or Noah."

"For you?" She asked dumbly.

Before she could think of anything else to say, Janet leaned forward and kissed her on the mouth. Claire sucked in her breath and held her hands up to the other girl's shoulders to hold her off. "Wait a minute."

"Yes, I know. It's wrong, but I can't help how I feel. You told me that you loved me, too." Janet sobbed.

Things began to click in Claire's mind. Were Faith and Janet lovers? Did that kind of thing happen back in the 30's? Had Faith been forced to marry a man, when she had in fact been in love with a woman? That would certainly explain her parents' threat of disowning her. They must have found out about the affair and wanted to end it the only way they knew how.

"Do Faith's...I mean, do my parents know about us?"

Janet looked confused but shrugged. "What do you mean? You're the one that told me they did."

Claire suddenly wished she had brought the diary with her. She really needed to find out what had happened the last few months of Faith's life. She sighed and then took a deep breath.

"Let's just go about our evening, alright? There are better places for us to talk."

Janet nodded and walked to the mirror. She wiped her eyes and checked her makeup and hair. Claire remained where she stood and gazed at her reflection. It still freaked her out to see Faith staring back at her.

They met the men at the concession stand. Noah held the drinks and Hank had the popcorn. "Are you ladies ready to go in? The movie should be starting soon."

Claire nodded, taking the proffered drink from Noah and then walking past him into the theater. She gasped when she entered. She hadn't known what she expected, but it wasn't what she saw. Theaters had definitely been much nicer and grander back in the 30's than in her time. She felt they should be watching an opera instead of some silly western.

They walked toward the middle of the theater, and she sank into the plush seat. She took a sip of her drink and frowned at the strong taste of the cola. The lights dimmed only a few minutes later, and she sat back to enjoy the show. A few cartoon shorts and a newsreel started first, and Claire watched the news with interest. She had never cared much for history, but it interested her to see it first hand. The current president, FDR, discussed the economic crisis and how he hoped his new Social Security law would help. Claire then realized she had been sent back to the middle of the Great Depression. She did remember the stock market crash of 1929, which had been only six years earlier. She racked her brain trying to remember when the worst of the depression hit and thought it might be 1933. Her mind wandered during the rest of the newsreel, and then *Hopalong Cassidy* started.

An hour later it ended, and she fought laughter. "They call that a movie? It was only an hour long."

Only Janet heard her as the men stood and awaited them in the aisle. "It's Intermission, Faith. The next one will start in a few minutes."

Claire smiled as they headed out, actually thankful for the intermission. The short movie had been a bit corny. A cowboy dressed all in black that didn't smoke or drink and always tried to do the right thing…and he made quite a contrast on a white stallion. Claire personally felt he should have had a black horse. She wondered if the second movie would also only be an hour. "Who names their horse Topper?" She asked under her breath with a smile.

They all went to the restrooms and got more snacks before heading back into the theater. Claire still felt full from the first batch of popcorn so didn't have anything else. Luckily, the second movie ended in just over an hour and then they were back outside. They had already eaten, so Claire hoped the night would be over soon. She wanted to get back to her house and read Faith's diary. She also wanted to be away from Hank. She had just been forced to sit beside him for over two hours and had tolerated enough of his company.

Hank and Noah talked nonstop about *Hoppy Cassidy* the entire way back. Neither Claire nor Janet contributed to the conversation, but the men didn't seem to mind. Claire just stared outside the window, looking for familiar surroundings.

Once they got back to the house, Janet told Claire that she would see her Saturday morning and then left. Noah had his own car, so he wished them all a fine evening. When she faced Hank alone, Claire had to fight to keep from bolting toward the front door. She clasped her hands in front of her as Hank walked her to the porch.

"Can I kiss you goodnight, Faith?" He asked.

"I'd prefer if you didn't," she responded honestly.

He frowned and ignored her response, leaning forward. She turned her head at the last minute, and he kissed her cheek for an instant before she stepped away and opened the front door. "Good night, Hank!" She wished she knew his last name. She had read it in the article but couldn't remember it. Claire closed the door behind her and leaned against it. Maybe that would be in the diary as well. She looked toward the stairs, before racing up them to Faith's room.

Chapter 7

Claire curled up in Faith's bed with her diary and began to read. She started with an entry in March 1935 and read until the end. Faith hadn't been a frequent visitor to her diary, which might explain why she'd been writing in just the one since she turned eight. The average entry could be anywhere from one week to a full month apart. She wrote very small as well, so her entries were generally at most half a page.

Just about every entry contained some mention of Janet. Claire's eyes widened slightly as Faith revealed the first time Janet kissed her. It had been a relatively innocent kiss after Faith's seventeenth birthday party. The kiss and the feelings associated with it confused Faith, and there hadn't been another entry for a month. She regretted asking her mother if kissing Janet had been a wrong thing to do. Margie had been horrified, and Claire winced as she continued to read. Faith had been told not to have any more dealings with Janet, but the teenager had tearfully refused. They were best friends after all and had just made a little mistake. She had promised her mother that it would never happen again. She asked Margie not to tell her father about the incident and could only hope she had kept her promise not to.

Janet and Faith always went to the movies on Friday nights, and they kissed again one night in mid June. Knowing the wrongness of it, they both had been in tears afterwards. Faith didn't want to go against her mother, especially since she promised her that it would never happen again, but she couldn't control the feelings that grew within her. She could no longer look at Janet as just a friend. She loved her, and practically had since they first met. Janet and Faith had been friends since Janet's family moved into the neighborhood when she was only ten. They had met at the playground and had bonded instantly. How could the love they shared be wrong? Neither knew where their forbidden love could go, as both were inexperienced virgins.

Being a very good girl, Faith went to her mother about her serious problem. Expecting her mother to be furious at her, she didn't expect to see sadness in her face. She could tell she had disappointed her but didn't know what to do, but her mother said she would take care of it. Of course, Faith hadn't expected her solution.

The entries came more frequently starting in July. Faith had met Hank on the 4th of July, and several entries a week began in August. The couple became engaged on August 6th, and Claire cried as she read that entry. Margie told Faith that if she didn't agree to marry Hank, she would disown her and have her shipped off to boarding school. Faith would never see Janet again, but if she agreed to marry the man, Janet could continue to be in her life as a friend.

"Quite a fast courtship." Claire muttered while flipping to the next page. She couldn't help but wonder why Hank would want to marry a girl after only knowing her for a month. Faith obviously hadn't liked Hank. She never used his name but referred to him as "the man".

With only a few entries left to read, Claire noticed Noah had never been mentioned. Faith must surely have met him, but she had obviously not felt him worth writing about. Claire shook her head with a sigh. The poor girl had been too blinded by her love for her friend and hadn't realized what she missed out on. Being a lesbian would surely not have been an easy life in the 30's, and her mother obviously tried to protect her daughter the only way she knew how. Claire shook her head sadly at such a tragic end result. She had to confront Margie to put a stop to the wedding. At least being sent to a boarding school would save Faith's life. Claire couldn't help but wonder why Faith hadn't realized that once she turned eighteen, she could do what she wanted.

Though being in a depression, Faith probably knew she couldn't support herself. Not to mention she most likely valued her parent's opinion above all else. Why else would she marry a man she disliked? Though Faith did try to get out of the wedding the last few weeks of August, begging her parents to reconsider. She tried to convince them of the poor choice they had made in Hank. She tried to make them see that he hid something within himself, and that he scared her. Her parents said her love for Janet had clouded her opinion of him, and that they were well suited.

Claire read the last entry with new insight. No wonder the girl felt it impossible to ever love Hank. That last entry had been the only time Faith actually put his name in her diary. She sighed as she got out of bed and put the diary back in its safe place, closing the desk before going back to bed. Claire couldn't get to sleep at first. She dreaded what was to come. She knew she had to do it, but it wouldn't be easy. Claire did have the advantage of not loving Margie and Hector Pruitt. She had been sent back to accomplish one thing, and that was to stop Faith's marriage.

She stared at the ceiling, wondering if she would be able to go home after accomplishing that. She had read books on time travel but didn't know how it would work. She knew that in some of the stories, the heroine remained in the past. Claire cringed at the thought. Even though Faith had a perfectly healthy body, did she really want to spend the rest of her life in it? Claire then wondered about Faith. Did they switch places? Was Faith's mind in Claire's body?

Claire shook her head. She didn't think so, but she couldn't be sure about anything. If she went home, would Faith just think she had blacked out for the amount of time Claire had been in her body? If Claire went back, would it be to the exact time she left, or would it be the amount of elapsed time spent in 1935?

Realizing that her head began to ache, she told herself to stop thinking about it. She had enough to deal with without having to worry about that as well.

After a restless night, Margie knocking on the door awakened Claire. The door opened, and Claire opened her eyes.

"Your father and I would like to see you in the drawing room, young lady."

Claire closed her eyes with a groan. That didn't sound good. She nodded, and the door nearly slammed shut.

She got out of bed and pulled on Faith's robe, before heading downstairs. Not knowing where to go, she soon discovered the drawing room was actually the living room. Claire walked into the room to find both Margie and Hector sitting across from each other.

"You wanted to talk to me?" Claire asked them. Margie gestured to the seat beside her. Once she was seated, Hector spoke.

"I just received an unpleasant call from Hank. Apparently you were rude to him last night. Is that true, Faith?"

"Rude?" She asked with a lump in her throat.

"Yes, rude, and I would like you to explain yourself. You're marrying the man in a week, and we both expected you to be on your best behavior."

Margie contributed with a scolding tone. "You were doing so well. What happened?"

Claire shook her head, speechless at first. She needed caffeine in the worst way, being way too tired to deal with conflict first thing in the morning. She noticed both parents were fully dressed.

"I don't know what he's talking about. I just gave my opinion, and I guess he didn't like it."

"Your opinion on what?" Hector asked gently.

"I told him that I didn't like sailing."

Margie frowned. "How do you know you don't like it? You've never done it."

Yeah, and I don't need to eat shit to know I wouldn't like that, Claire thought with a smile.

"What's so funny?" Margie asked with a frown.

"Nothing's funny...Mother. Nothing about this whole situation is funny."

Margie stood and smoothed her skirt before looking down at Claire. "Don't mess this up, Faith. Hank is from good stock, and he will provide well for you. Just you think about the alternative before you're rude to him again. Is that clear?"

Claire looked across at Hector, who gave her a sad expression. "Listen to your mother, Faith. She knows what's best for you."

Claire almost challenged that comment but bit her lip instead, realizing she must bide her time. She had a week before she needed to rock the boat. Claire slowly nodded.

"OK, I'll try not to be rude to him. I'm sorry." She wondered what Hank would do if she overdid the niceness. What if she came on to him? She couldn't overdo it or he would run to the Pruitts, but maybe she could find out more about him that way. Her mother always told her that she could get more bees with honey than with vinegar. Claire bit her lip, wondering if she could stomach flirting with a man that made her skin crawl.

She nodded, deciding that she should at least try. She would definitely need to do something to help her avoid Janet. Claire didn't want to hurt the girl, but she definitely wasn't willing to act like she loved her.

"Good, since he's coming over for brunch. I want you to be on your best behavior."

Claire fought the cringe and nodded again. "Yes, Mother, I'll be good."

"Then go upstairs and get dressed. I want you to wear that blue dress I just got you. That will look the prettiest in your portrait."

Claire's eyes widened, having forgotten all about that. "What time will the painter be here?"

"Eleven o'clock, which will give you plenty of time to eat and socialize with your fiancé." Margie responded before heading out of the room. "Since he now knows about it, he might even want to stay and watch."

Claire rolled her eyes before looking back at Hector. He had noticed the gesture and frowned. "I just don't know what's gotten into you lately, Faith.

You aren't even the same person." He shook his head. "Guess I really am losing my little girl."

She had the strongest impulse to hug the man. He clearly didn't want Faith to get married, but he let his wife have her way. "Don't worry about me...Dad. I'll be fine." She assured him before leaving the room and running back upstairs.

Chapter 8

Claire sat at Faith's vanity and brushed her hair. Due to the way it had been styled, Claire had no idea of the loveliness or length of Faith's hair until she took it down for the first time. It fell in brown waves a few inches below her shoulders. Claire looked in the mirror and smiled at the reflection. She wished she had a bit of makeup to accentuate Faith's pretty blue eyes but then realized that Margie would probably have a fit.

The blue dress she wore flattered Faith's small frame. Compared to her own height of 5 feet 6 inches, Claire guessed Faith to be about 5 feet 2 inches tall. Of course, the three-inch heels made her taller. Claire grimaced as she looked down at the shoes. She had never liked wearing anything but flats or sneakers, but at least Faith's feet were used to them. She stood before the full-length mirror and smiled. As she visualized the painted portrait in her mind, the smile left her face. Faith looked so lost in that painting, and Claire wondered what the girl had thought about. Probably how miserable she would be in a loveless marriage. She bit her lip and wondered if she should smile for the sitting. Hank would probably be there, so she doubted she would want to.

Claire shook her head in wonderment. Since the painting seemed to be the key that unlocked the door to the past, maybe Claire herself sat for the one she had found. Maybe it hadn't been Faith who looked so lost. Claire sighed, fearing that would be another question she would never know the answer for. Why bother even trying to figure any of it out? Theoretically she shouldn't even be there at all, let alone sitting for someone else's portrait.

Sighing heavily, Claire left the room and headed downstairs. She met Margie on her way upstairs, and the older woman started as she saw her.

"I knew that dress would suit you…but what have you done to your hair, Faith?"

Claire put a hand to her head. "What's wrong with it?"

Margie frowned and shook her head. "Well, no time to fix it now. Hank just arrived, so I came to fetch you." Faith's mother sighed as she turned to descend the stairs, "and you knew today you were being painted."

"I think I look fine, Mother."

Margie clucked her tongue in disapproval but didn't say anything else. They reached the landing and headed for the dining room. Hank stood as they entered, and Claire sighed deeply. She had hoped that Noah would be there as well, but he was nowhere to be seen. She forced herself to meet Hank's gaze with a smile. "Hello, Hank."

"Good morning, Faith. I hope you are in good spirits today?"

She almost glared at him, knowing he meant to say better spirits. She couldn't help but think of how childish it had been for him to run crying to the Pruitts about her behavior the night before. She forced a bigger smile.

"Just peachy, thanks!"

Hector frowned over his daily paper before disappearing behind it again. Claire almost giggled as she approached the table. Hank pulled out her chair for her, and she nodded her thanks before being seated. He sat across from her as Margie took the seat opposite her husband.

No sooner had they all seated that the doors opened, and servants carried in several trays of food and placed them in the center of the table. Claire watched distractedly as they filled glasses with water and juice. She reached out and took a sip from her own water, staring at Hank over the top of the glass.

She had so many things she wanted to ask him but didn't feel comfortable doing so in front of Faith's parents. "So, will you be staying for the portrait?" She asked him.

He had just put a bite of sausage into his mouth, so he held up his hand and nodded. Claire fought a grin, since she had waited until he had a full mouth before speaking. Once he had swallowed, he cleared his throat. "Sorry…yes, of course, I'd love to stay."

She nodded. "It will probably be quite dull. Maybe you should ask Noah to come over to keep you company?"

Hank's frown was subtle. "You should be company enough, Faith."

Margie cleared her throat loudly. "Yes, you two can chat during the sitting. Should make it less *dull* for you, dear." She finished, giving Claire a warning look.

Claire nodded and licked her lips. "Yes, right, how true."

Claire shifted uncomfortably in her seat for the rest of the meal. Margie and Hank carried most of the conversation, but he shot Claire odd looks on occasion. She wished she could just melt through the chair. Hector remained hidden behind his paper throughout most of the meal, finally putting it away when his coffee was served to him.

"Well, I'll be at the club most of the day!" He stood and kissed the top of Faith's head. "Have fun with your portrait, my dear." He then kissed Margie on the cheek and shook Hank's hand. "See you later, my lad."

They all watched him leave and then left the dining table. Margie led the way into the sitting room. "Well, I'll just be sitting in the corner working on my needlepoint. You two have a nice chat."

Claire watched her walk to the corner and sit in a chair about fifteen feet away. She continued to stare until Hank spoke.

"I guess I should apologize." He said a bit sheepishly.

Claire's eyes widened as she turned to stare at him. He gestured to the couch beside them, which faced the fireplace. She smiled, sparing a glance at Margie and realized they were being chaperoned. Her mind raced, wondering how she would ever get any information from Hank, if they could never be alone.

"About what?" She asked as they sat upon the couch.

Hank sighed and took her hand. Claire used every bit of control within her to keep from pulling it from his grasp.

"I shouldn't have called your father this morning. If we're to be married, we need to communicate with each other. I should have sought you out and discussed the problem with you."

Claire nodded. "Yes, you're right, but I'm also sorry. I shouldn't have been so rude to you last night." She stole a glance at Margie and lowered her voice, "and I really think we need to find some time to be alone, to really get to know each other."

Hank's eyes widened as he too looked at Margie. His eyes narrowed slightly, and he looked back at Claire. "Would that be such a good idea?"

"We're to be married in a week, right? How wrong can it be to want to spend some time alone together?" She could tell when his mind had sunk too low, and she shook her head at his leer. "I mean away from my parents...and away from Janet. Maybe Noah could be our chaperone?" She licked her dry lips.

Hank sighed. "Well, Noah *is* staying with me until after the wedding."

"He's staying with you?" She repeated.

"Yes, he and his family don't live here…didn't I tell you that before?" He asked with a deepening frown.

Claire shrugged. "You might have, but I've been a bit scatter brained lately…with planning the wedding and all."

That appeared to appease him, and he nodded. "Yes, I can see how that might affect your memory." He stared at her intently. "I just wish I knew where all this was coming from. Ever since you met me, you've barely spoken to me…only answered when a direct question was asked of you."

Claire's mind raced as she thought of Noah. She hadn't expected that he stayed with Hank. "My mother and I had an insightful chat, and I realized that I need to mend my ways… but you just need to keep this between us. I know my parents wouldn't approve. I would just like to see where you live and feel comfortable there. After all, won't I be living there soon?"

"OK, Faith, after I leave this afternoon, tell your mother you want to go visit Janet. I'll pick you up around the corner."

Claire smiled triumphantly. Without Janet and the Pruitts around, maybe she could learn more about both men… though she was more interested in getting closer to Noah.

"Thanks, Hank, you won't regret it."

The painter positioned Claire in a high backed chair in front of the living room's fireplace.

He then opened all the windows to let the light in. She watched Hank and Margie sit across the room as the painter fussed with Faith's hair. Claire watched Margie purse her lips together and smiled, reminded of how she hadn't liked her hairstyle. Claire didn't know what was wrong with it. She had left it long and loose, feeling that would look nicer in the portrait. The painter pushed some stray strands behind her ear and fluffed it up a bit.

"OK, move as little as possible, young lady," he instructed and began to set up his easel. He pulled out the brushes and paint, and Claire wished he had done all that before making her sit in the uncomfortable chair.

"How long should this take?" She asked.

"Not too terribly long," came his quick response before he dove behind the canvas again. Quite a few minutes later, he finally sat and began to paint. The minutes passed by slowly. Margie spoke up occasionally and told her not to slouch in the chair, and Claire pulled herself up against the back again. Every once in awhile, she looked at Hank, who stared at her curiously. She forced a grin and quickly looked away.

Neither Margie nor Hank spoke that often, more interested in watching the painter. Claire really tried to smile for the portrait, but that soon chipped away, and she found herself yawning.

After awhile, she let her mind wander. She thought about the irony of finding a portrait in an attic and feeling that it called to her, and how she ended up sitting for that very painting. Claire frowned as she thought about Faith's fate. She would die tragically in just over a week, if Claire didn't stop it. She wondered if she failed, would she die as well or be transported back to the 21st century? Her gaze slowly traveled back to Hank. She would have to play her cards right, or she could very well die by his hands. Both she and Noah could die. She then realized she might be there to save both their lives. She pictured Noah's face, and a sad smile faintly touched her lips. Could she do it? If Hank were truly a monster and had killed his wife and best friend, could she stop him?

"That's the expression I was looking for!" The painter blurted suddenly, bringing Claire's thoughts back to her surroundings. She looked toward him but only saw the canvas. When he peered around it again, slight disappointment shown on his features. "Well, I think I captured it well enough, though I doubt you could recreate it anyway."

Claire frowned, wondering what he went on about. She looked at Margie and Hank, both of whom stared at the portrait. Margie held a handkerchief to her watering eyes.

"It's so beautiful," she muttered, clearly trying to hold on to her emotions.

Hank looked a bit haunted himself as he stared at what the painter had done. Claire wondered if he would finish soon. Her butt ached, and she needed to walk around.

"Are you almost done, or can I get a break soon?"

"Faith, behave!" Margie called from across the room.

"I am, Mother, but this isn't the most comfortable chair in the house." Claire responded with a groan.

The painter frowned at her but nodded. "I am almost done. Just a few more finishing touches."

Claire rolled her eyes and shifted on the chair. If he didn't finish soon, she might just stand up and leave. What's the worst that could happen? She nearly giggled over that thought and the mental image that crossed her mind. Margie would be mortified and be sputtering in shock and outrage, but what could she really do? She already planned to marry Faith off to a man she didn't like. Claire grinned as that image kept her seated.

"Voila!" The painter finally announced. "C'est fini!"

Claire knew enough French to know that he had finished. "Thank God!" She said with a sigh of relief and stood to stretch. She ignored Margie's look of disapproval as she joined them in front of the portrait. Claire gasped as she set eyes on it.

"It's exactly the same!" She said aloud without thinking.

"What's the same?" Margie asked with confusion.

"I…uh…I just meant I dreamt it would look like this. Amazing," she muttered to herself as she continued to stare at Faith's portrait. The hair, the haunted eyes and expression, all were exactly the same as in the painting Claire had found in the attic.

She again looked at the hair and shook her head. "That's not how my hair is." She said and looked at the painter.

He shrugged and pointed to Margie. "Your mother told me to go with a more popular style."

Claire didn't even look at Faith's mother, her gaze returning to the painting instead. Tears filled her eyes, finally knowing what had fueled that lost look on Faith's face. Without knowing she did it, Claire stepped closer to the painting. It still seemed to call to her, and she held out her hand to touch the painted cheek.

The painter jumped forward to block her, guarding his new masterpiece. "You'll ruin it! A painting should never be touched, especially when it's still wet!" He admonished her.

Claire gasped and jumped back as if burnt. Margie took her hand and pulled her aside, "What has gotten into you, Faith? I raised you better than that." She then approached the painter, expressing her apologies at her daughter's ignorance. Claire shook her head, backing away, unable to take her eyes off the portrait.

Chapter 9

Once alone in Hank's car, Claire began to wonder at the sensibility of her plan. She gave him a sideways glance and bit her lip. She supposed she should feel safe enough until the marriage, but he still made her extremely nervous.

Their meeting had gone off as planned. Margie had no problem with her visiting Janet after Hank left, though her expression did show a hint of disapproval. Of course, Claire knew the reason, so she had merely smiled reassuringly at Faith's mother and told her they wanted to work on the wedding plans.

"I've never seen your hair like that before," Hank's voice broke the silence in the car.

Claire looked at him sharply, her hand involuntarily moving up to Faith's hair. "Oh? Is that a good or a bad thing?"

He looked toward her with a grin that made her uncomfortable. "Oh, it's good. Makes you look older…more mature."

"Why do you want to marry me, Hank?" Claire asked quickly, before she lost her nerve.

He frowned at her. "What kind of question is that?"

"I'm curious is all. You haven't known me long enough to love me."

Hank took a deep breath before looking back toward the road in front of them. "I need a wife, and you come from a good family."

"Why do you need a wife?"

Hank frowned again. "Every man needs a wife, Faith. How else will I have children to pass on my name?"

"How old are you?" She asked suddenly.

He gave her a sideways glance. "I'm twenty-five."

"Will this be your first marriage?"

Hank shifted uncomfortably in his seat, but he didn't look at her. She noticed his clenched jaw and wondered if she should stop asking him questions.

"Will it?" She repeated against her better judgment.

Hank gave her a sharp look that surprised her but quickly disguised it with a sigh. "I just don't understand where all these questions are coming from, Faith. What's going on?"

Claire bit her lower lip and shook her head. "Nothing, I just wanted to get to know you a bit better. Maybe I don't feel I know you well enough to be marrying you and wanted to rectify that."

Hank didn't speak for a few moments and eventually pulled the car over and parked on the curb. Claire looked outside the window, and her eyes flew open. The mansion had to be at least three times larger than the Pruitts' house.

"Where are we?" She asked in wonder.

"My home…and soon to be yours," he added almost reluctantly.

Claire whipped her head around to meet his gaze with a frown of her own. A smile suddenly broke out on his face, and he patted her arm. "You wanted to see it, right?"

Her frown deepened, but she nodded. "Yes, I did…Is Noah here now?"

Hank looked toward the house with a shrug. "Can't tell from here." He met her gaze again. "Why so interested in Noah all of a sudden? Until yesterday, I hadn't thought you realized he even existed."

She licked her dry lips. "I'm trying to mend my ways. I realize I haven't behaved properly since we met."

Hank chuckled. "Oh, Faith, we both know why, now don't we?"

He left her looking confused as he opened his door and got out of the car.

Claire stopped in the foyer and looked around in awe. "Don't you have some kind of garage attached to this mansion? Kind of surprised you parked on the street."

Hank grinned with a shake of his head. "It's not a mansion, Faith." He looked around the room before adding, "someday though." As if remembering her first question, he shrugged. "I don't like dealing with driving all the way around the house to get to the garage. Easier just to park out front."

Claire suddenly wished that if Noah were there that he would make his presence known. She didn't relish the idea of spending anymore time alone with Hank. She had asked what he meant by his last comment in the car, but he had just shaken his head and hadn't answered.

A man appeared out of nowhere, and Claire started. She relaxed after realizing she had met the butler, though she had hoped it would be Noah. She watched the man take Hank's coat and hat.

"Thanks, Sanders. Have you seen Noah around?" Hank asked the man.

Sanders gave him a quick nod. "Yes, sir, Mr. Palmer is in the pool." With that said, he went back to wherever he came from.

"You have a pool?" Claire asked in envy, having always wanted a pool. Her therapist said that swimming would be the best thing she could do for her hips and legs, but her family couldn't afford a built in one. They had an above ground pool, but her handicap made it too hard to get inside. "Is it built in?"

Hank gave her a confused look, and Claire realized that he might not know anything about above ground pools. She certainly didn't know when the first one had been publicly offered! She shook her head quickly with a laugh. "Ignore that! Stupid question, but you do have a pool? Can I see it?"

"Sure, follow me." He shook his head as if dealing with an idiot and led the way to the back yard. "Is it built in?" He repeated softly in a mocking tone.

Claire glared at his back as they left through the back door. She nearly whistled as she gazed around. "You sure this isn't a mansion, since it certainly looks like one?" A large deck surrounded the huge pool, which overlooked the grass and trees beyond, and a small cottage stood about twenty feet off to the left. To the right beyond the huge yard, she saw the two-story garage with its driveway disappearing around the side of the house.

"Maybe it's a mansion by your estimation, but I can assure you that this is rather a small estate by standard measures." Hank replied with a surly tone.

Claire looked away from him with a sneer and noticed Noah leaving the pool. The water ran down his bared chest, and she couldn't take her eyes off the shimmering bronze skin.

Hank followed her gaze and waved to his friend. Noah waved back and grabbed a big towel from a nearby chair. He blotted his chest and then wrapped it around his lean hips.

They met him on the deck, and Noah smiled at Claire.

"Nice to see you again, Faith."

Claire nodded. "And it's nice to see you as well, Noah."

Noah glanced behind them before giving Hank a questioning look. "Is it just the two of you?"

Hank nodded with a chuckle. "Yes, Faith here wanted to see my home. She asked if you could be our chaperone."

Noah laughed and looked at Claire with a friendly grin. "That's not exactly proper, now is it?"

She returned his contagious smile with a shrug. "Maybe not, but I don't care. I trust you."

Noah raised an eyebrow and looked at Hank, who turned to stare at Claire.

"Well, I would hope you trust me as well?"

Claire cleared her throat with a wince, realizing she shouldn't have been so open with Noah. She nearly choked on her reply, since she hated to lie. "Of course, Hank."

Hank sighed and shook his head. He turned to look back at Noah. "How's the water?"

Claire stayed outside with Noah, while Hank went to his room to change into his swimming suit. At first they had all planned to go inside to chat, but Claire told Hank that he should swim if he wanted to. She wished to be alone with Noah for a while anyway, so she jumped on the chance. Hank had reluctantly agreed and had left them alone.

"You sure you don't want to come in? I think there might be a few extra swimsuits in the pool shed," Noah suggested, pointing to the cottage behind him.

Claire smiled at his shed reference and returned her gaze to him as she shook her head. "I don't swim much. Thanks, though." She sat on a lounge chair beside where he stood. "So, how long have you known Hank?"

Noah looked toward the main house in thought. "We went to boarding school together…I guess I first met him when we were sixteen."

"Wow, that long? So are you the same age?"

Noah sat beside her and wiped his hands down his towel covered legs. He winked at her. "Is that your covert way of asking my age?"

Claire had to hold in the giggle. She just hoped her hot cheeks didn't mean she blushed. She didn't know what it was about the man, but he made her feel like a schoolgirl. True, Faith may be only seventeen, but Claire was a twenty-six year-old woman. She was older than Hank, for goodness sake! She did let a smile slip through as she nodded.

"Yep, we're both twenty-five." He placed his arms behind him and gripped the sides of the lounge chair, leaning back slightly. "You're really pretty when you smile. You should do it more often."

Her eyes widened slightly at the unexpected compliment. "It's easy to smile when in good company."

Noah looked at the house again before returning his gaze to Claire. "Anymore questions, Miss Faith?"

Claire nodded. "Tons…are you married?"

He chuckled and shook his head. "No one's snared me yet."

"What about Hank?"

The smile melted away, and Noah sat forward with a shrug. "He doesn't like to talk about his first marriage. Didn't end well, I think."

Claire frowned, looking at the house, hoping that Hank had trouble finding his shorts. "What do you mean?"

Noah shook his head. "I met her a few times, even went to the wedding back in '29, but then they moved away. I actually haven't even seen Hank that much in recent years, and when I asked about her, he just said it didn't work out. I didn't want to pry, so I dropped it." He gnawed on his lower lip and looked deep into her eyes for a moment. "I'm pretty sure that's how he was able to buy this place though."

"What do you mean?" Claire repeated.

"Don't you two look cozy?"

Claire and Noah looked up with a start. Hank had just cleared the threshold of the back door and halted when he saw them sitting so close together.

Claire looked him up and down. He had an open robe over his gray shorts. Where Noah looked like a sun God, Hank's pale and hairless chest made him look almost like a ghost.

Noah laughed and stood. "Dang, man, you need to spend more time out here. Get some color on you."

Hank smiled at him as he approached, taking off his robe and tossing it over the back of Claire's lounger. "Maybe I'll take that bit of advice. It definitely looks good on you."

He kicked off his deck shoes and stared down at Claire. "Did I miss something? You two looked deep in conversation?"

Claire shook her head. "Just passing the time with idle chit chat."

Hank nodded and looked at Noah. As if sensing Hank needed confirmation, he also nodded.

"Just keeping your fiancé occupied while you were inside. You ready to get wet?" Noah finished with a smile. He took off his towel and then dove into the pool. Since she stayed on the lounger, the two men pretty much ignored her the rest of the time they spent outside. She didn't mind though, since she had time to go through what Noah revealed to her.

Chapter 10

Claire stretched out on the lounger, lost in thought. When the water splashed upon her, she looked up in surprise. Hank stood beside her chair and stared down at her. The expression on his face seemed so familiar that she found herself openly returning his stare with wide eyes. She frowned as it felt like an old memory fought its way to the surface.

"What's wrong? You look as if you've seen a ghost?" He asked.

Claire had a brief flash of déjà vu but couldn't be sure what it meant. There had certainly not been any other time she had been in the position to be lying beneath a standing Hank, but it still made an unpleasant chill go down her back. She sat up on the lounger, swinging her legs to the deck.

"I'm fine," she sputtered, still a bit spooked by the feelings he had brought forth within her. Claire looked beyond him to see Noah pulling himself from the pool. He smiled at her as their gazes locked. She swallowed the lump in her throat and tried to smile back.

"You should have come in, Faith. The water is so refreshing," Noah said with a sigh. He grabbed his towel from the nearby chair and swung it around his damp shoulders. Concern flashed across his gorgeous features as he knelt beside her.

"You look so pale. Are you alright?" He looked ready to touch her forehead, but he held himself back, turning to look at Hank. "Maybe we should all go inside?" He asked his friend.

She shook her head and cleared her throat, still wondering about the sense of déjà vu she had experienced. What had it meant? "I'm fine," she repeated.

Hank held out a hand to her. "I think sitting out here in the sun wasn't a good idea. Maybe I should be getting you home."

"I said I'm fine." She responded, staring at his hand. She didn't want to touch him, so she pushed herself off the chair and stood between the two men.

"Phone call for you, Mr. Holmes." The voice behind them startled Claire, and she turned to stare at the butler.

"Thanks, Sanders, I'll be right in." Hank told the man before he looked at Noah. "Why don't you show her to the living room, and I'll join you in a few minutes."

Noah nodded as Hank set off toward the house. Once he had gone inside, Claire looked at Noah, who gazed at her with genuine concern.

"Are you sure you're alright? You did go quite pale there."

Claire slowly nodded as she let her gaze wander across his face, from his eyes to his nose and mouth and then up to his damp hair.

"You keep looking at me that way, and I just might blush." Noah said with a soft chuckle.

Claire blinked as she looked back at his eyes. "What do you mean?" She asked, even though she realized she shouldn't have been staring at him like that. A small smile touched her lips. She looked beyond him at the pool, wishing for different circumstances. She would have liked it to be just the two of them. She could be wearing a sexy bikini and be showing off for Noah, flirting with him in the water.

"Maybe I should have borrowed a suit. The water might have done me some good."

He followed her gaze and nodded. "Next time then?"

She looked at him and cleared her throat. How could this man consider someone like Hank a friend? She wanted to be alone with him, so they could talk privately. She had many questions and didn't even know if she should ask them. How could she be sure that he would keep her questions to himself? Though something inside Claire told her that she could trust Noah. "I hope there is a next time," she finally answered.

Noah grinned before gesturing toward the house. "Shall we?"

She nodded and followed him to the living room. Claire looked around as they walked through the house, finding it hard to believe that Hank lived there all alone.

"So Hank never had any children from his first marriage?"

They had just entered the living room, and Noah turned at her question. He shook his head. "He's never spoken of any."

Claire looked around the room, not too surprised at not seeing any photos. "How long has he owned this house?"

Noah didn't answer at first. "I'm not sure. Maybe you should be asking Hank all these questions?"

Claire licked her dry lips. "I feel more comfortable talking to you."

He frowned. "Why?"

She wanted to reveal everything to him in that instant, knowing full well that she couldn't do it. She finally shrugged. "I just feel a connection to you."

Noah shifted the slightest distance closer to her and looked a bit bewildered. "Before yesterday, you had never even looked at me…but when you smiled at me in the car last night…" He trailed off, looking slightly uncomfortable.

Claire took a step closer. "Yes?" She prodded.

Noah sighed and shook his head. "It's hard to describe, and I don't really think I should."

"Why not? I'd like to know what you were going to say." She looked up at him, fighting the temptation to place her palms on his chest.

He shook his head with a soft groan. "Before yesterday you were just a kid that was being forced to marry my friend, but when you smiled at me…well, you seemed like someone else…more mature…a woman." He sighed, "I'm not making any sense."

Claire nodded quickly. "Yes, you are." His perception amazed her.

Noah looked at her with soft smile. "I had never seen you smile before last night… let alone at me."

A lump formed in her throat, and she nodded again. "I guess I didn't have good reason to smile before."

"Why would I give you reason to smile?" He asked quietly, looking as if he dreaded the answer.

Claire gazed up at him and licked her lips. He watched the movement and sighed softly. "You're marrying my best friend," he whispered.

"Am I?" She responded mysteriously, and surprise registered on Noah's face.

He took a few steps away from her and shook his head. "What are you saying?"

Claire looked over his shoulder as she heard steps approaching. "Ask me again sometime."

"Sorry about that," Hank said as he walked into the room. "Now, where were we?" He looked from Claire to Noah. Claire shrugged and sat on the couch, reluctantly looking at Hank. Once she met his gaze, she flinched as what Sanders had said echoed inside her head. *Phone call for you, Mr. Holmes.* Hank's last name was Holmes? It took Claire a moment before she realized why that name sounded familiar, and she stared at him in shock.

"What's wrong with you, Faith?" He asked, crossing the room quickly so that he stood directly in front of her, staring down at her with a look of disdain. The expression brought forth the same déjà vu she had experienced earlier, and she stood up with a gasp, edging away from him.

"It was you!" She accused him, fighting the urge to run away. She looked at Noah in a panic, involuntarily moving closer to him.

"What's wrong?" He asked her, his eyes widening at her frightened look.

It couldn't be happening, she told herself, unable to resist looking back at Hank, who now looked at her with a confused expression.

Claire couldn't possibly be standing in front of the same man that had run her down with his car when she had been sixteen. As she stared at Hank and tried to visualize him as an old man, everything snapped into focus. She suddenly remembered the old man's first name, which had been Hank... Hank Holmes. With that realization she began to sink to the floor in a dead faint, but Noah caught her before she fell, sweeping her up into his strong arms.

Chapter 11

"What was she doing there?"

"You'll have to ask Hank."

At first Claire didn't recognize the voices but then realized that Janet and Noah spoke. She groaned and opened her eyes. Janet sat on the edge of the bed and looked away from Noah to stare down at her friend.

"Faith, are you alright? Noah says you fainted." She took her hand and squeezed it.

Claire looked around the room, but she didn't see Hank. She turned her gaze back to Noah and smiled.

"Did you carry me in here?"

He nodded. "Are you alright?"

Claire returned the nod and looked at Janet. She must be in her bedroom, and Noah had carried her in and placed her on Janet's bed. Claire wished she had been conscious to enjoy being in his arms. "Where's Hank?" She asked with distaste.

"He stayed home. He wanted to bring you himself, but since you passed out in my arms, I figured it made the most sense to take you myself."

Claire smiled at his choice of words: *take you myself*. "I'm glad it was you."

"What happened, Faith? Why were you there? It was so improper." Janet asked in a scolding tone.

Claire sat up with a shrug. "I just wanted to see if I could find out anything about him." She scowled as she remembered what she had uncovered. "It worked too well, though." She coughed and cleared her throat. "Can I get some water? My throat is awfully dry."

"Oh yes, of course." Janet patted her hand and then stood to leave the room. "I'll be right back," she added with a glare in Noah's direction. As soon as she left the room, Noah moved closer to the bed.

"What did you mean it worked too well?" Noah asked, pulling Janet's desk chair with him to sit beside her. "I saw your expression before you passed out. You looked at Hank as if he were some kind of monster. I actually think that's why he so readily let me leave with you. I doubt he wants to see that expression again anytime soon."

Claire looked into his eyes and licked her dry lips. "Well, I don't want to see him anytime soon either." She so badly wanted to tell him everything, but she couldn't. He would think her insane and have her locked up. Faith certainly deserved a better future than that. Tears misted the corners of her eyes. "I don't know what to do now, Noah. I didn't expect this."

His features softened at seeing her tears. Noah reached out and caressed her cheek. "Don't cry, Faith. We'll figure it out."

"Maybe you should go, Mr. Palmer. I think that Faith has had enough excitement today and needs her rest."

Noah jumped back as if burnt and turned to see Janet in the doorway holding the glass of water. Claire tried not to look guilty, but she could feel the heat blooming in her cheeks. Noah nodded and stood, pushing the chair back to the desk.

"You're right, Janet. She does need her rest." He looked at Claire. "I hope you feel better soon, Faith."

Claire swallowed the lump in her throat and nodded. "Thank you, Noah."

She watched him leave the room, closing the door behind him. Claire then looked at Janet with a sigh. The girl gave her a hurt look.

"What did you find out about Hank that made you faint?"

"He was married before," she stammered, not knowing what else to say.

"Why would that make you faint?"

"Because I have the feeling that he might have killed her." The thought hadn't entered her head until Claire actually said it. He killed Faith, so that could very well mean he had killed his first wife as well. Hadn't she read that Hank had been married five times? Claire suddenly wished she had done more research on him but hadn't realized then that she had been doing research on just one man instead of two.

She still couldn't wrap her mind around the fact that Hank had been the one to hit her with his expensive car. She could now clearly see the old man glaring down at her and then looking at his car with concern. That meant the evil bastard lived a very long life, and it just didn't seem fair.

"What do you mean?" Janet asked with a gasp. "How could you possibly know that?"

Claire shook her head. "I didn't say I knew. I said I had the feeling he did." She cleared her throat, reaching for the glass that Janet still held. She took a long drink of the water. "I just know that Hank is a very bad man, and I am suddenly not sure how to get away from him." She bit her lower lip to keep it from trembling.

Janet sighed and wrapped her arms around her. Claire allowed the embrace, actually needing the comfort of another person. She would have preferred to be in Noah's arms, but she knew that couldn't happen…no matter how much she wanted it to.

"We'll figure something out, Faith. I promise." Janet soothed, stroking one hand down her friend's hair.

Claire nodded and closed her eyes, trying to block out the memory of Hank glaring down at her.

Claire spent the rest of the day at Janet's, whose parents had been out when Noah carried her in earlier. They arrived a few hours later and insisted on Claire dining with them. Janet's mother had even made the phone call to Margie to let her know of the invite. Claire enjoyed her time with them and absorbed as much information as she could. After dinner, Janet's father pulled out his brand new Monopoly board game and asked if everyone wanted to play. It had taken a moment for Claire to get over her surprise, not knowing that the game had been around in 1935. She watched them set it up, very interested in seeing how it differed from the version she grew up playing. The smile left her face as the game reminded her of her own family, all of whom she missed very much. She told Janet's parents that she needed to go home.

Claire left the house and returned to her own, pushing Monopoly and her family from her thoughts. She let Janet do most of the talking while she had been in the girl's home, trying to learn as much about their friendship as she could. Since Faith only used the diary every once in a while, much of their relationship was unknown. She just felt thankful that Janet hadn't attempted to kiss her again, though she had found out a few necessary things.

Faith's senior year of high school would have started that coming Monday, and Janet expressed her sorrow that they wouldn't be graduating together. The Pruitts felt it unnecessary for Faith to finish high school, since she would be marrying a wealthy man. That appalled Claire, even though she knew Faith wouldn't live to graduate anyway. Even if she intended on changing it, Claire wondered about rocking that boat. Should she insist that Faith attend her final year of high school? Her lip curled at the thought of having to waste her time sitting in class. The wedding took place in exactly a week, but if she changed the future, did she really have to pay attention to dates? In the original history Faith died in ten days, so Claire could only assume she had to get past that date, or how could she be sure she stopped the murder? Claire didn't know what she should do next.

How could she even pretend to be friendly to Hank? At first she only suspected him of murdering Faith and Noah, but now she realized he had almost killed her. Feeling a bit overwhelmed, she tried to ignore her feeling that he might have killed his first wife as well. Hank truly was a monster, and she didn't want to be around him at all. Claire shook her head. Maybe she shouldn't ignore the feeling that he had killed his first wife. Maybe she needed to prove it and have Hank punished for the crime. Being in jail would ensure both Faith's and Noah's safety. Claire bit her lip, not knowing how she could prove such a thing. She swallowed the lump in her throat, realizing that in order to find out more about the first wife, she would have to continue being nice to Hank. Claire sucked her breath in through clenched teeth and shook her head, not knowing the possibility of niceness toward him. Even Noah had noticed how she had looked at Hank. Surely Hank had noticed as well. Maybe he wouldn't even want to marry her anymore. What would Faith's parents do, if Hank were the one to call off the wedding? Would they still disown her? Claire smiled as a thought occurred to her. What if she acted unbearable around him? Did he want a wife badly enough to marry a shrew?

Claire sighed. What did he care, since he planned to kill her shortly after the wedding anyway? She rolled her eyes at her own stupidity and stared at her own house ahead of her. She had been walking slowly, dreading going back in there and facing Margie. Claire wondered if Hank had tattled on her again. She wished to be back in the 21st century, where she could walk in there and not have to worry about the Pruitts or Hank…or Noah. She sighed as she thought of him. She would never see him again if she went back, and that thought truly saddened her. Claire had never met a man like him before, one that could make her blush just by looking at her. He made her feel warm inside, and she absently thought of what his lips would feel like against hers. Claire didn't know how much time she had in the past, and she truly wanted to get better acquainted with him before being sent back.

She smiled as a thought crept into her head. Noah had known Hank's first wife. Maybe he could help her find out more about the woman. As another thought surfaced, Claire stopped walking and her jaw fell open. If she stopped Hank from killing Faith and Noah and possibly got him arrested for the murder of his first wife, that might stop him from becoming that rich old bastard that had run her down with his car. Could that be possible? Could that be the ultimate reason she had been sent back, to save her own future?

Chapter 12

Claire entered the house and looked around, wondering if the Pruitts lay in wait for her. Should she get the confrontation over with or just hide upstairs in Faith's room? Claire sighed, not knowing which would be preferable. Margie took the decision out of her hands by stepping over the threshold into the living room.

"Did you have a nice visit with your *friend*?" The older woman asked, enunciating the last word with barely disguised loathing.

Claire winced before nodding. "Yes, it was quite pleasant." She felt rooted to the spot, not sure which way to go, like a deer caught in headlights.

"I didn't think you would be spending the whole day there. What if Hank had wanted to spend some time with you?"

"I think I've spent enough time with him, Mother."

Margie frowned then deeply sighed. She gestured toward the room behind her. "Come inside, Faith. I would like to talk to you."

Claire bit the inside of her lip as she nodded, slowly following the older woman into the living room. She sat across from Margie and placed her hands in her lap, waiting for Faith's mother to begin.

"I'm worried about you, Faith."

"What are you worried about?" Claire asked with a bit of nervousness.

Margie studied her face for a moment before responding. "Well, you're not acting or talking like yourself…and since when do you call me Mother? You never sassed me before either. I just don't understand what's going on."

Claire sucked air through her teeth and sighed. She had read Faith's diary and knew very well what she called Margie, and she regretted ignoring that bit of information. "I guess I decided that if I'm to be a married woman, I need to stop calling you such a childish name."

Margie frowned and pursed her lips together. "You're not married yet, Faith."

"You're right, Mum, and I'm sorry." Claire responded in a soothing tone.

"I know you don't want to get married, Faith, but I hope that someday you'll understand why it's necessary."

Claire's eyes widened. "Oh, I know exactly why you want me to marry that monster. You feel that is a better fate than being branded a lesbian."

Margie stood with a shocked gasp, covering her mouth with a shaking hand. "Why would you say such a terrible thing? How could those words come from my daughter's mouth? I didn't raise you to sass me like this."

"Maybe cause you didn't raise me," Claire muttered under her breath.

"What was that, young lady?" Margie asked in a rising voice.

Claire stood and held up her hands. "I don't think you raised your daughter to condemn her to such a fate."

Confusion replaced the shocked expression on Margie's face. "Condemn you? How can being married to an upstanding man be condemning you?"

"Did you know he's been married before?" Claire answered with another question, which shocked Margie into silence. Claire continued, "and it didn't last, but I don't think it ended in divorce."

Margie sighed. "Has he actually told you of his past or are you just making all this up to shock me?"

Claire shrugged with a smile. "Whichever works."

"There's no talking to you, is there?" Margie asked in resignation. "Do you think all this nonsense will change my mind about your marriage? Well, it won't."

Numerous scenarios went through Claire's mind. She could flat out refuse to marry Hank and suffer the consequences, or she could act like she agreed with Margie until the wedding approached and then run away. If she chose the latter, where could she go? Noah's face sprang to mind, and she wished she knew where he lived. She didn't even have a way of getting in touch with him. He planned to stay with Hank until after the honeymoon, but what if she could convince him to go home early?

"I'm going to school with Janet tomorrow," she said quickly.

Margie only stared at first before slowly shaking her head. "We've already decided that's not necessary. Besides, you're not even registered!"

"I think you decided. I doubt I had much say so in the matter, but now I've decided I want to go to school." Again Claire's mind raced. She didn't actually want to go to high school, but anything would be preferable to sitting about the Pruitts' home and wondering what to do about the following weekend. "Doesn't matter anyway. I registered myself," she lied.

Margie gasped and placed a hand to her heart. Claire frowned to see tears fill the older woman's eyes. "I just don't know you anymore, Faith." She took a deep breath and sighed. "Do whatever you want this coming week, but accept your fate. You will be a married woman on Saturday and will have to do what your husband asks of you."

We'll see about that, she told herself as she smiled at Margie. "Whatever you say, Mother."

Her gaze suddenly caught sight of the abstract painting above the fireplace, still surprised not to see Faith's portrait. "Where's my painting?" Claire asked with a frown.

It took Margie a moment to adjust to the change of subject, and her frown went far deeper than Claire's. She shook her head and took a deep breath, following Claire's gaze. "It's been wrapped. After all, it *is* a wedding present for Hank."

Claire cringed, "but where is it?" She pressed.

Margie looked away from the fireplace to glare at her daughter. "It is of no concern at this time. It will be in your new home soon, and you can worry about it then."

Claire wanted to push the subject but decided against it. She couldn't leave before she stopped Hank, but her mind would rest a bit easier if she knew the portrait's location. She bit her lower lip in thought. She didn't know but could only hope that touching the painting would send her back home. Since she truly felt it was the gateway between the future and the past, Claire slowly nodded. "I'm tired. I think I'll go to my room now." She looked up at Margie with a smile. "Good night…Mum."

With that she turned and left the room, leaving behind a very confused and troubled woman.

Claire awoke early the next day and did her best to fix her hair in the current style. She thought she failed miserably, but Margie's smile rewarded her as she entered the kitchen.

"You look lovely, Faith."

"Thank you, Mum." Claire responded in a rehearsed tone of voice. She had fallen asleep repeating the word Mum over and over again. She certainly never called her mother that, so she hadn't been used to the word. It seemed to please Margie, who began to place different food items on the breakfast nook. Claire decided she needed to help her, and when Mr. Pruitt came in, they all had a nice meal together.

Claire left the house shortly after Faith's father did. Margie handed her a bagged lunch and told her to have a good day. Claire thanked her with a smile and then headed for Janet's house. She shook her head, wondering how she would explain the situation to Faith's friend. She waited outside Janet's house until she saw the teenager exit the front door.

Janet's eyes widened to see her. "Faith, what are you doing here?"

Claire took a deep breath and then proceeded to tell Janet her plan. They walked along the sidewalk, and Janet slowed to a stop a few blocks away from her house.

"Why did you lie to your mother about going to school?"

Claire shrugged. "I just needed an excuse to be out of that house to think. I'd never be able to do anything as long as Margie is lurking around."

Janet frowned slightly. "You've never called your mother by her first name before," she noted softly and began walking again.

Claire fell in stride with her, looking ahead of them. "How far away is the school?"

"About a mile but don't change the subject."

"Which was?" Claire asked with a grin, and Janet chuckled in spite of herself.

"So you're going to walk to and from school with me, so your parents think you're attending…but what will you actually be doing?"

Claire thought about it, absently kicking a pebble on the sidewalk. How could she tell Janet, when she didn't exactly know what she would be doing? "I know I want to do some research on Hank, so I guess I'll start at the library." She knew well enough to leave any mention of Noah out of her plans. Janet had enough suspicions and jealousy already. Claire didn't even know how she would get Noah alone or go about finding him. She certainly didn't remember where Hank lived. She silently cursed herself for not paying better attention when he drove her there.

When the two girls reached the school, Janet turned to face her, clutching her notebooks to her chest. "Well, I'll miss you. Try to stay out of trouble?"

Claire grinned at the teenager. "I'll try," she responded with a wink.

"And you'll be here when school lets out?"

Claire nodded and asked Janet what time that would be. "I'll be here, and we can walk home together." She gnawed on her lower lip for a second before stepping closer. "I'll need your help this week, Janet. I'll need you to summarize what you learned, in case I'm questioned."

Janet nodded. "Of course I'll help you." Taking advantage of having Claire close to her, she leaned forward and gave her a quick peck on the lips, before turning and racing toward the school steps. Claire looked around, relieved they had been behind a bush where no one could see them.

She sighed and turned away from the school. She knew the library would be in the same place, since it had been over a hundred years old in her time. Realizing she would need to walk wherever she wanted to go, Claire took off down the sidewalk.

She hadn't gone a mile, when she sensed a car pacing her. Feeling a moment's fear that Hank found her, Claire forced herself to turn and look instead of fleeing. She almost couldn't believe what her eyes told her. She stopped walking and stared at him through the passenger side window.

"Noah?"

He leaned over and pushed open the door. "Get in, Faith."

She stared at him in shock for a moment but then did as he asked. Once seated, she looked at him in confusion.

"What are you doing here?" She asked him.

Noah looked at her as if trying to decide something. He finally shrugged as he pulled the car away from the curb and drove down the street. "I saw you leave school and decided to see where you were going."

Claire frowned, "but what were you doing at the school?"

"I followed you and Janet there."

"You followed us? From my house?" She waited for his nod. "But why?"

Noah muttered something under his breath and shook his head. "I shouldn't have let you see me. I could have followed you all day, and you wouldn't even have known it."

"What are you talking about, Noah? Why were you following me?"

He looked at her with a hint of indecision in his expression and licked his lips.

"I can see you don't want to tell me, but you have to. You can trust me." She coaxed him, placing a hand on his arm.

Noah looked down at her hand for a moment before meeting her gaze. "I don't know why I know that, but I do." He took a deep breath and then nodded. "Following people is what I do, Faith. It's my job."

She frowned. "What do you mean it's your job?"

He slowed the car at a stop sign before turning to look at her again. "I'm a private investigator, Faith. I was hired to find out what happened to Hank's first wife."

Chapter 13

Claire stared at Noah in shock. "You're kidding," she gasped but then realized that it made a bit of sense. Had that been why Hank had killed both Noah and Faith? Had he discovered his friend's hidden agenda? Claire shook her head in bewilderment, "you're not kidding."

Noah didn't respond as he turned to look back at the road in front of them.

"But you're his friend," she whispered, smiling in spite of herself. She had wondered how he could truly be friendly with a guy like Hank.

He gave her a sheepish grin. "We used to be friends. Like I said, I hadn't seen him in years. Tina was such a sweet girl. Her parents needed someone that Hank would trust. It took a bit of convincing, but I agreed to help them find out what happened to their little girl." He finished with a sigh.

"He killed her, didn't he?" Claire asked softly.

Noah nodded. "It was ruled accidental of course, but yes, Tina's parents think that Hank killed her." He gave her an intense look, "and so do you."

Her eyes widened, but she couldn't deny it. Tears filled Claire's eyes, and she quickly wiped them away. She took a shaky breath and nodded, "and I'm pretty sure I'm next, which is why I can't marry him."

Noah suddenly pulled the car to the side of the road and turned to her, putting a comforting hand on her arm. "I'm not going to let anything happen to you."

Claire felt fresh tears fill her eyes as the newspaper headline flashed across her mind. It had read *Newlywed and Best Man die in tragic boating mishap*. Noah's fate would be the same as hers, unless they were able to change it. She licked her dry lips and tried to nod. "I'm glad you trusted me with this, Noah. I want to help you." She looked deeply into his eyes and felt herself getting lost in them. The strong magnetism between the two brought them closer without either of them being aware of it. In the next instant they were kissing. Even as the shock of the situation gave way to passion, Claire wrapped her arms tightly around him.

She didn't know which of them ended the kiss, but she stared breathlessly into his eyes. Claire arms still encircled his neck, and she could feel his hands on her back. Neither could speak at first, and Claire had to fight the urge to reclaim his lips. She blinked a few times before pulling slightly away from him.

"How did that happen?" She moved one of her hands to her mouth and then licked her lips. She could still taste him and nearly moaned. Claire had never dreamt that a kiss could be that good. She felt warm all over, especially between her legs. Claire blushed at the thought of being turned on, which had never happened to her before.

Noah shook his head, the passion slowly ebbing out of his eyes. As he became aware of her in his embrace, he pulled his arms back and faced the road, putting his hands on the steering wheel. He cleared his throat and took a deep breath. "Oh, my God!" He whispered.

"What's wrong?" She asked through the fingers still in front of her face.

"I shouldn't have done that." He finally looked at her. "I'm sorry, Faith. That was inappropriate of me."

Claire gasped with a smile. "You? I was a part of it as well." She dropped her hand before boldly replying, "and I'm not sorry at all."

Noah frowned slightly. "Are you sure you're only seventeen?"

She almost laughed aloud but didn't answer him. Instead she cleared her throat and smoothed her skirt. "Maybe we should talk about how we're going to work together to find out what happened to Tina?"

"I really don't want you involved in this, Faith. You could get hurt."

Claire bit her lip as she returned his stare. How could she tell him that was why she was there? She had to change the future and save them. Working with Noah would be the only way she could do that. "You don't want me doing this on my own, do you?"

Noah's gaze narrowed and his lips pursed. "You wouldn't?"

"I would," she responded with a sly grin. "Why don't you just tell me what you've uncovered so far? After all, you've been staying at Hank's house."

Noah sighed before pulling the car back onto the road. He shifted on his seat a few times and cleared his throat. "Hank is very secretive. There are several locked rooms that I haven't been able to get into yet, and he doesn't leave me alone long enough to do too much snooping."

Claire could see his discomfort and wondered if their kiss had affected him as much as it had her. "Have you brought up Tina to him at all?"

"I tried, and he refused to talk about her. Said it was too troubling to him."

"Troubling my ass!" She said without thinking. Noah shot her a surprised look that soon clouded with suspicion.

"What is going on with you, Faith?" He asked in a troubled voice.

"What do you mean?" She asked nervously

He shook his head. "I noticed it Friday night! You aren't the same girl I first met. Something is going on with you, and I just wish I could figure it out. I'm trusting you, so why can't you trust me?"

Claire swallowed the lump in her throat and licked her suddenly dry lips, wishing she had some water. "Maybe cause my secret is a bit harder to reveal."

Noah nervously chuckle. "What secret could a teenager have?"

She met his gaze for a moment, knowing that Faith did have her own secrets. Claire wondered if Noah knew about Janet. She had the feeling that Hank either knew or suspected. She hadn't pressed him on the subject when he drove her to his home, but his tone had suggested he knew something that he shouldn't. Claire wondered if he had told Noah, which would further confuse him since they shared such a passionate kiss. Her breathing grew shallow as she remembered how good his tongue had felt in her mouth and how she had wantonly suckled him. She quivered and tried to force her mind from the memory. Noah noticed her reaction and frowned.

"What is it? It can't be that bad."

Claire nearly laughed at his misinterpretation and wanted to set his mind at ease, but how could she? She certainly couldn't reveal where her mind had been just then. Claire could feel her cheeks getting warm and hoped they weren't as red as they felt. Needing to change the subject, she looked out the window. "Where are you taking me?" She asked suddenly.

"My office." He answered distractedly. She could tell he wanted to continue their discussion and didn't appreciate the new topic.

Her eyes widened. "You have an office?"

Noah smiled, and her heart nearly melted. "Tina's folks rented it for me. I certainly can't keep anything at Hank's that he might find or trust that my phone calls are private."

Claire nodded. "That makes sense. Is it anywhere near the library? I wanted to do some research today."

"Actually, it's right across the street. I knew I would need it for research as well."

"Great," she beamed at him. "Maybe we can research together."

Noah stopped at his office first and checked his messages. Finding out that he had a secretary surprised Claire.

"Good morning, Mr. Palmer," the petite blonde smiled her greeting.

"Morning, Nancy, any calls?"

She nodded and handed him a few slips of paper. Claire watched him sort through them as he gestured to her. "This is Faith Pruitt. Faith, this is my secretary, Nancy Davis."

Nancy looked at Claire with a surprised expression before she gave her a beaming smile. "Well, it's nice to meet you, Faith. I've heard a lot about you."

Noah shot his secretary a sideways glance that made Claire smile. "Nice to meet you, too, Nancy. Unfortunately, I can't say that I've heard of you. I just learned today what Noah does."

Nancy giggled. "Yes, don't you just love the spy business?"

Noah placed a hand at the small of Claire's back and gave his secretary a mock glare. "We'll be in my office, Nancy."

"Yes, sir!" She replied with a wink and a smile.

Noah closed the door behind them, and Claire turned to him with a grin. "Now, I like her." She said with a chuckle.

"Courtesy of Mr. Baltimore."

She raised her brows at the name.

"Hank's father-in-law. He has tried to cover all the bases, and Nancy has been a huge help. If anyone comes in here and inquires, she has an entire rehearsed speech about who rents this office. Mr. Baltimore is extremely wealthy and knows how to get what he wants."

"Too bad he let his daughter marry Hank." Claire responded, the smile leaving her face.

Noah suddenly placed both hands on her shoulders and drew her within a foot of his face. "I want you to trust me, Faith. I need you to trust me."

His nearness made her breathless and speechless as her gaze went to his mouth. She pulled her lower lip between her teeth and licked it, the tip of her tongue poking out to lightly touch her upper lip. Noah followed the movement and then closed his eyes, his grip tightening on her shoulders.

"I do trust you, Noah," Claire whispered huskily. She didn't know what it was about this man that made her want to wrap herself around him. No other man had ever affected her that way, though she hadn't had much experience in her life. She was as virginal as the body she currently occupied.

Noah opened his eyes and their gazes locked. His blue eyes shimmered with longing. "Then please level with me. What is it about Hank that you know? Why does he scare you?"

She frowned, wondering what to tell him. "I'll tell you this much. He plans to kill me after the wedding…and I think he figures out you're against him. We're both in danger, Noah." Claire finished and clutched his shirtsleeve. "I don't want anything to happen to you."

Noah's frown rivaled her own. "Is this based on fact or speculation?"

"Let's just say that it's both, and that we can change our fates…we *have* to change them." Claire suddenly got nervous. What if she couldn't save them both? Should she get any more attached to him, knowing that he could be dead in little over a week? She shook her head, knowing full well that it was too late for that. She could already feel herself falling for him. She didn't even know how that could be possible after only four days. Claire had certainly never believed in love at first sight, but then she had never felt this way before. One of her last conversations with Stefanie about soul mates suddenly surfaced in her mind. If she ever met that special person, she thought her feelings would be how she felt for Noah. Claire moved a hand up to touch his cheek. Had she traveled back through time to meet him? Confusion flooded her mind, as she no longer knew the primary purpose. Was it to save Faith and Noah, bring Hank to justice or meet her soul mate? Could it be all of them? Could there be other reasons as well? Could she hope to achieve any of them let alone them all?

"Why are you crying, love?" Noah whispered, moving a hand to her face to wipe the tears away.

Claire hadn't been aware of crying, but she quivered at the endearment and the caress. Without another thought, she melted into his arms, and his lips seared her own. Her fingers went into his thick hair as she deepened the passionate embrace.

Noah's hand crept to her bottom, and he pulled her against his body with a groan. She gasped to feel his hardening flesh between them. Claire pulled away slightly and looked into his eyes. She couldn't think let alone speak and didn't know how far it would have gone, if not for a knock at the door. Claire pulled away from him with a small squeak and looked down at her clothing. Everything looked in order, and she glanced up to see Noah run his hands through his hair. He quickly moved behind the desk and sat down, before turning toward the door.

"Come in."

Nancy walked in and looked from Noah to Claire. She smiled at Claire before walking over to the desk and handing Noah a piece of paper. "I thought you'd like to see this."

He looked at what she had given him before nodding. "Thanks, Nancy."

The secretary nodded and turned to leave, but she gave Claire a wink as she passed her. Claire blushed and looked away. Silence followed the door closing behind the secretary. A few moments later Claire finally met Noah's gaze. He stared at her with an unreadable expression.

"You said you wanted to do some research at the library?" He asked softly.

She blinked a few times, thrown off by the subject change. She bit her lip and tried to control her expression, not wanting to reveal her disappointment to him. Claire nodded slowly.

"Why don't you go ahead? I have to do some work and then I'll come over to fetch you. I suppose you'll want to be back at school when it lets out?"

Claire nodded again, but a frown slipped through. "How can you act like that didn't just happen?" She asked in spite of herself.

Noah looked at the top of his desk and sighed. "Maybe because I can't believe it happened. I'm a grown man who should be in better control of his impulses." He looked up to meet her gaze, and she sucked in her breath. The longing in his eyes made her mouth fall open. "What is it about you, Faith? I feel as if I could lose myself in you, and I can't afford to do that. I'm here to do a job, and I can't have such a distraction."

She swallowed the hurt. "That's what I am, a distraction?"

Noah groaned and stood. He looked ready to walk around the desk toward her, but he held his ground. Grasping the back of the chair, he shook his head. "You're far more than that. You said you feel that Hank means to kill you, and that I may be in danger as well. If any of that is true, I need to have my wits about me. How can I do that, when all I can think about is burying myself inside of you?" He groaned again and closed his eyes. "I don't think we should be alone anymore. You're just too much of a temptation."

Butterflies erupted in her stomach and flew downward at his words. She got warm all over and couldn't hold back the smile. It pleased her to know that she affected him as much as he did her.

His eyes opened and met her gaze. "I'm glad to hear that you don't mean to marry Hank." He shook his head, "though if we can prove he killed Tina, there isn't much chance of him marrying anyone ever again."

Doubt shadowed her face as what he said sunk in. If he could prove Hank killed Tina, the marriage wouldn't happen, but it had happened. Hank had gotten away with killing both Faith and Noah, and he married three other women and lived a long life. It just didn't seem fair. "What if you can't prove it?" She managed to choke out. "What if he gets away with it and comes after me?"

Noah didn't answer at first. "Then I'll kill him myself."

Chapter 14

Claire sat in the basement of the library and stared off into space. Her fingers lightly tapped the pages of the huge archive that lay spread open in front of her. She didn't know why she had expected neatly ordered microfilm and had been slightly surprised to see that all the old newspapers had been bound into huge books. Claire had only gotten about half way through her first volume, when her shared kiss with Noah leapt into her mind.

She could still feel how his lips had pressed against hers, taste his tongue and feel his hard body melded against her own. Claire suddenly shook her head. It had been Faith's body that had fit so well, not her own.

"Damn," she muttered under her breath, feeling her lower lip tremble with emotion. Claire closed her eyes and licked her dry lips. Had it been Faith responding with passion, or had it been her? She shook her head. Faith loved Janet. Claire suddenly wondered what the teenager would think about Noah kissing her. Realizing that things were getting very complicated, Claire tried to focus on the newsprint in front of her. It would take forever to find anything, but she couldn't give up.

"Any luck?"

The masculine voice at her ear nearly made her yell. Claire spun around and faced Noah, slightly surprised to see him standing just behind her chair.

"How did you sneak up on me?" She asked with a gasp.

Noah smiled at her and shook his head. "I didn't sneak. Though you did seem really absorbed staring at that wall."

Claire felt herself blush, wondering how long he had been in the basement with her before he spoke up. She frowned and watched him walk around the table and sit across from her. "Any luck?" He repeated, staring at the archive between them.

Claire followed his gaze and shook her head. "There's so much to look through, and I'm not really sure what I'm looking for. I don't even know when Hank got married."

Noah chuckled. "You could have asked me."

She couldn't respond and stared into his expressive eyes. Claire slowly nodded, pulling her lower lip between her teeth. Noah watched the movement before meeting her gaze.

"Don't I need to get you back to the school?" He asked softly.

At first the question didn't register in her mind. Claire blinked a few times and stared across the room, finally noting the clock. Her eyes widened to see how much time had passed, and she hadn't accomplished anything. "Yes, that's right." Claire closed the archive in front of her. "How time flies when you're having fun," she commented sarcastically. Noah smiled as he stood.

"Shall we?" He held out his hand, indicating the stairs behind her.

Claire nodded but didn't move. "Did you get a lot of work done today?"

Noah looked as if he didn't want to answer but nodded instead. "A bit, though not as much as I would've liked."

Claire looked down at the table in front of her, almost afraid to speak. She cleared her throat. "Where do we go from here?" She finally asked.

"What do you mean?" Noah responded after a moment's pause.

She looked up at him with a smile. "You know what I mean. Things have changed. I left the house this morning thinking I had to do this on my own. Now I know I have an ally." Claire took a deep breath, focusing on the lunch bag Margie had prepared for her that morning. A lunch she had forgotten to eat. Claire licked her dry lips, forcing herself to meet Noah's gaze. "Things have changed between us. Don't try to deny it."

Noah sighed and shoved his hands into his pockets. "You are direct, aren't you?" He shifted slightly before nodding. "Yes, of course, things have changed between us, but that's not the most important thing here, is it? We both want to expose Hank, though our motives are different."

Claire frowned when he stopped talking. To keep from having to look at him, she concentrated on the ignored lunch. She realized she was hungry as she opened the bag to peer inside. Her lunch consisted of a sandwich, a muffin and an apple. Claire grabbed the muffin and pulled it out of the bag to get a better look. She smiled to see the blueberries. It was one of her favorites, though lemon took the grand prize in that department. She held it up in front of her. "I forgot to eat."

Noah stared at the muffin for a moment before looking back at her face. "So what's the plan, Faith? Am I to pick you up at the school each morning and then drop you off later in the day? Is that what you had in mind?"

Claire took a small bite of the muffin before returning his gaze. "I thought you would be here earlier to help with the research. What have you been doing all day?"

Noah sighed and ran his hands through his hair, a gesture that Claire had become quite fond of. She smiled in spite of herself, wishing it were her own hands going through those silky strands. Claire shook herself to concentrate on their conversation.

"Mr. Baltimore had a few errands he wanted me to run." Noah began with a slight groan, and Claire could tell they hadn't been productive. He shook his head. "Of course they were dead ends. Hank covered his tracks well."

Claire shook her head in frustration. "He must have slipped up at least once." She looked at the archive on the table. "When did he marry Tina? When did she die? Am I even close?"

Noah followed her gaze and then shook his head. "You're a bit off." He reached forward and opened it, flipping some pages. "You've got the right year there but the wrong month." He closed the book and sighed. "You can find it tomorrow. I need to get you back to the school."

Claire looked at the book with a bit of irritation. What she wouldn't give for a computerized list that she could search. It would take forever to find out anything about Hank in such an archaic system. Claire almost laughed at her own reference. It was 1935, not the dark ages, but it still felt as medieval. She looked up at Noah with a playful grin. "I think I'm in the wrong century."

He smiled back, of course not fully comprehending her joking reference. "Aren't we all?"

They didn't talk much during the car ride back to the school. Claire gnawed on her cuticles, not caring they weren't her hands. She had much to consider after such an enlightening day. When she awoke that morning, she never would have dreamt the day would have turned out as it had. She had kissed Noah not once, but twice. Her stomach flipped over just thinking about it. Claire gave him a sideways glance as she thought about how well they had fit together. She couldn't help but think how the sex would be and licked her lips in anticipation. When she realized where her thoughts headed, Claire gasped softly and forced her gaze out the passenger window.

"So you'll pick me up same time tomorrow morning?" She asked softly, hoping she didn't sound as anxious as she felt.

Noah's response didn't come as soon as she would have liked. She turned to stare at him as he sighed and nodded. "Yes."

Claire looked down the street and noticed Janet standing on the curb a few blocks down. She held up her hand to Noah. "We don't want her to see us together."

Noah turned the next corner and pulled the car to the curb. "Can Janet keep this to herself?" He asked as he turned toward her.

Claire shrugged. "I think so…as long as she doesn't know you're helping me." She paused for a moment as she remembered something he had mentioned at the library. "You said I had the right year, but the wrong month. Did Tina die shortly after she married Hank?"

Noah frowned at the question before slowly shaking his head with a sigh. "It was almost a year later, but let's worry about that tomorrow. Janet is waiting for you."

Claire returned the frown, suddenly sensing that he wanted to be away from her. "What is going on, Noah? I feel you're keeping something from me." She then remembered what he had said in his office about not wanting to be alone with her anymore. She wanted to ask him how Tina had died, but she also wanted to ask him other things. She wanted to know how he felt about her and if he liked kissing her. He had called her a temptation, but he also called her a distraction. Did he think of her as a kid, even though he had treated her like the woman she truly was?

She swallowed the lump in her throat, realizing he had been right to keep her on track. She may be in 1935 for several reasons, but the most important ones were to stop Faith's death and to stop Hank from killing anyone else. Everything else needed to take a back seat for now. Claire returned her gaze to Noah, who had stared at her in silence.

"You look like you just made an important decision." He noted.

"I did. OK, Noah, we'll play it your way. Tomorrow you'll tell me when Hank got married and when Tina died. I can do the rest on my own."

Noah shook his head. "You don't have to do it on your own, Faith. I just..."

"Don't worry, Noah," she interrupted. "I understand... and I agree. We both need to concentrate on what must be done. We're running out of time." Without another word, Claire opened the door and jumped out of the car. She ran around the corner before Noah had the chance to respond.

Claire slowed to a walk before Janet turned toward her. She approached Faith's friend with a smile and a wave.

"Any luck?" Janet asked, when she stood beside her.

"Not much, so I'll be going back tomorrow to look some more."

Janet appeared disappointed. "So you'll be spending the whole week at the library?"

"If I need to," Claire responded. "You can't expect me to attend class with you?"

Janet shrugged. "I guess not. I just miss you, Faith."

Not knowing what else to say, Claire said the first thing that came to her mind. "Well, you'll miss me more once I'm gone."

Janet's eyes widened. "What do you mean, gone?" She asked with a gasp.

"I meant married, silly." Claire responded with what she hoped was a smile, but the frown deepened across Janet's face.

"I thought you said you weren't going to marry that man?"

Claire cursed silently at her blunder. "I don't intend to, but who knows if I can really get out of it. My mother seems pretty determined, and you know how she can be."

Tears filled Janet's eyes as she hugged her books tightly against her chest and lowered her chin with a nod. Claire went with her instinct to comfort the girl and rubbed her back. "But I'll keep looking at the library. Maybe I'll find something to use against him."

That seemed to cheer Janet a bit, and they headed for home. Claire listened to what had happened that day in school, forcing herself to pay attention whenever her mind would begin to wander. When they reached their houses, Claire kept her distance as they said goodbye, before turning and heading to her own home.

When she opened the front door to see Hank standing in the living room, Claire's surprised gaze went from him to Faith's parents.

"Hello, Faith. I hope you're feeling better?" Hank asked with mock concern.

Claire shot him a glare and shook her head. She then looked back at the Pruitts, who didn't seem concerned by the question. "What are you doing here?" She asked, shifting her gaze back to Hank.

"I thought it best to be honest with your parents. After all, they'll soon be my parents as well."

Claire slowly stepped into the living room, still unable to comprehend what was going on. "You were honest about what?" She asked through clenched teeth.

"About your visit to my home yesterday. We've been discussing your peculiar actions of late and have come to a decision."

"About?" Claire asked, the hair on the back of her neck standing on end. Her gaze went from Hector to Margie. The older woman nodded stiffly before standing beside her husband.

"We've decided to push up the wedding. It would be sooner, but Wednesday morning is the Father's first available appointment."

"What?" The statement came as such a shock, Claire moved backwards until she slammed against the nearest wall.

Chapter 15

"What?" Claire repeated again but louder. "You can't do that!" She shook her head, not expecting such a change in plans. Her mind raced. At least the wedding hadn't been planned for the following day, or she would be unable to meet with Noah. He would surely be able to help her get out of it. Couldn't he? Claire shook her head harder.

"Of course we can, Faith." Margie assured her. "We've already discussed this. You know it's for the best, especially after being in Hank's home without a chaperone."

"But we did," she stammered.

"Another bachelor? Not exactly proper, young lady, and you know that!"

"I'm not ready to be married yet!" Claire whined, cringing at her own tone. She sounded desperate, which was exactly how she felt.

A sigh brought her attention to Hector. Claire beseeched Faith's father with her eyes. "Please don't do this to me," she begged him.

Sadness crossed his features before he shook his head. "It's for the best, Faith. You've become unmanageable, my dear. Maybe being a wife will sort things out for you." He approached her. "I only want what's best for you in the long run." When he made to touch her, she jumped back as if burnt. She had been mistaken in thinking he might be an ally.

It seemed she only had Noah. The thought of him nearly made her groan. She had no way of getting in touch with him until the following morning. What if she couldn't make that meeting?

"No, this isn't what's best for me. It will be the end of me!" Claire nearly screamed.

Hector and Margie exchanged worried glances before looking at her as if she were a lunatic. Claire suddenly realized that things could get a lot worse for her if Faith's family thought she had lost her mind. She closed her eyes and took a deep breath, letting it out slowly.

"I'm sorry. Maybe I'm overreacting." She looked at Hank and had to fight the tears of rage threatening to fill her eyes. She hadn't had time to do any research, so she had no fuel to throw on the fire. She had no proof that Hank had done anything wrong. He had been a model citizen as far as the Pruitts were concerned.

She had to calm things down so that she would still be allowed to go to school with Janet on Tuesday.

"I think it's just the jitters," Hank contributed, slowly moving closer to Claire. "I've actually heard of that. Some brides have second thoughts and panic before they are married."

Claire swallowed the lump in her throat, forcing herself to remain where she stood. She allowed Hank to put a hand on her shoulder, but she refused to look at him. Instead she looked at Hector. "Maybe he's right. You all just took me by surprise. I thought I had until the weekend to prepare."

Her mind remained foggy for the next few minutes. Hank said his goodbyes and took Claire's hand to lead her to the front door. She bit her tongue to keep from telling him not to touch her but forced herself to meet his gaze. Hank lowered his face to hers, and she stared into his soulless eyes without flinching.

"I don't know what is going on in your head, Faith, but you must realize there is no way out." He whispered. "You will be my wife, whether you like me or not." Hank turned slightly to grab his hat from the coat rack. As he placed it on his head he gave her a speculative glance. "You can't possibly think your parents would let you end up with Janet?" He finished with a sneer before smiling and patting her shoulder. Claire's eyes widened slightly, but she didn't say anything. She watched him turn away and leave the house as she stared at the closed door in mute shock. Margie's sharp voice brought her back to her surroundings.

"Quite a display, Faith. I'm so ashamed of you. How could you act like that? I'm only thinking of your reputation. First that debacle with Janet and then spending time alone with two men? Do you wish to be the center of gossip?"

Claire could only stare at first as tears filled her eyes. She so badly wanted to tell Margie that so long as Faith lived, she didn't care what people said. Instead she bit her tongue and shook her head. "No, Mum, I'm sorry."

Margie's features softened, and she crossed her hands in front of her. "Now don't start crying. It isn't a death sentence, no matter how you want to look at it. Hank will do right by you, mark my words."

Claire then remembered how Mrs. Pruitt had held onto the house for years after she no longer lived in it and had rented it solely because Faith told her to in a dream. She remembered feeling that Margie must have felt guilty after her daughter's death. She had forced the marriage and had lost Faith on her honeymoon, doing something she never would have otherwise. For the first time Claire felt sympathy for Margie. The older woman truly felt her daughter would have a good marriage, never realizing what a monster Hank had been.

Claire nodded and wiped her eyes. "You're right. I'm just being silly." She gave Margie a bright smile. "Can I at least spend tomorrow doing what I want to do? After all, it's my last day as a child."

"What do you want to do?" Margie asked with a hint of suspicion.

"Go to school, of course. I promised Janet that I would help her with a project."

Margie sighed. "What's the point, Faith? We need to make the final preparations."

"I made a promise, and besides, what is there for me to do? This is basically an elopement, right? I just have to show up." She grabbed Margie's hand and pressed it to her chest. "Please, mummy?" She asked sweetly.

Margie rolled her eyes, but a smile broke through. "Oh, alright, but I want you home as soon as school lets out. No dilly dallying."

Claire nodded fiercely, feeling as if she had won a contest. "I won't…I promise."

It took her forever to fall asleep that night, but she awoke early the next morning. She got dressed, taking care with her hair and wardrobe. Claire didn't want anything to upset Margie and make her change her mind about letting her leave the house. Just thinking about the next 24 hours made her a bit nervous. She and Noah didn't have much time to find something that might convince the Pruitts that Hank was a poor choice.

Claire entered the kitchen and smiled at Margie, relieved to see a bagged lunch being packed for her. She breathed a sigh of relief as she approached the older woman.

"Are you sure you want to waste your last day in our home at school?" Margie seemed reluctant to hand her the lunch.

Claire licked her lips and nodded. "We'll have the rest of the day together. I just want to spend today doing something normal." She finished with a smile.

"Well, have a good day, dear, and remember to be home right after."

"Yes, Mum." Claire nearly snatched the bag out of Margie's grasp and made for the door. "See you this afternoon," she called over her shoulder and left the house.

"They what?" Janet squeaked when she had heard the news. "Tomorrow?"

Claire nodded, "so today is my last chance to find something on Hank. I no longer have the whole week."

Janet looked ready to cry, so Claire shook her head. "Don't worry! I won't marry him. I'll run away if I have to. They can't make me marry him, if I'm not there."

"You can hide at my house," Janet replied, brightening a bit.

"No, that's the first place they would look," Claire gnawed on her lower lip. The idea of hiding in Noah's office sprang to mind, but she couldn't say that out loud, at least not in front of Janet. She knew it was close to the library, so she could find it again, if she had to. Claire decided she would discuss that with Noah when she saw him.

Janet cringed. "Yeah, you're right." Frustrated, she kicked a loose stone in front of her. "It's just not fair!"

Claire fought the snort that wanted to erupt. She almost told the girl that nothing in life was fair, but she bit her tongue. "No, it's not."

They didn't talk much the rest of the way to school. Janet turned toward Claire once they reached the steps. "Well, I hope you find something on him today."

"I will…I have to." Claire stepped back and gave a half-hearted wave. "See you after school lets out."

Janet noticed the distance Claire placed between them and frowned. "Yeah, see you later."

Claire gave her a big grin and then began to walk away, feeling Janet's stare. She felt relief when she rounded a corner and was out of sight. Looking for Noah's car, Claire let out her breath in a rush. She didn't know how much longer she could put on an act for everyone around her.

As she stood on the curb Claire realized that she hadn't had much time to herself since being propelled to the past. She took a deep breath and looked around. She smelled the freshly cut grass in the breeze blowing through her hair. In spite of the chaos that had been shoved upon her it was a lovely fall day, and she stood there in a healthy young body. Claire smiled as she looked down Faith's dress to her slender ankles. She could never imagine just standing on a curb, as it would have been painful in her own body. Claire gnawed on her lower lip at the thought of what she would do to be back in that battered body. True, she missed her family and friends not to mention the luxuries of the 21st century, but she knew she would miss 1935 when she went back…if she went back. Claire tried to swallow the lump forming in her throat at the thought of going back, at never seeing Noah again. She licked her dry lips and cleared her throat. She knew that if she were being honest with herself that he would be the only thing she would truly miss when or if she went back, even more than she would miss being in Faith's healthy body. Faith deserved to have her body back, and she also deserved to have it for a full lifetime. Claire nodded, remembering that had been the main reason for being sent to 1935, not to fall in love.

A few minutes later Noah's car pulled up alongside the curb. Claire smiled at him and opened the door to slide in beside him. She didn't waste any time telling him her news.

"Oh, damn!" He breathed when she stopped talking. "That is an unexpected twist."

Claire gave a short bark of laughter. "No kidding." She shook her head. "That only gives us today to dig up something on Hank."

Noah nodded as he stared out the windshield. "Then we don't have a moment to waste." He pulled the car away from the curb and headed for the library.

The archives were in the basement, and they went down the stairs in silence. Claire could tell that Noah had a lot on his mind. She didn't want to pry, but she didn't like how awkward she felt with him. "So, when did Tina die?"

Noah looked at her with a shrug. "November of '29."

"And when did they get married?"

His lips moved up into a small smile. "Tina wanted a Valentine wedding."

Claire frowned, "so they got married on February 14th, and she died in November of the same year?" She absently noticed Noah nodding as she did the math in her head. "That's nine months. Why did he wait so long to kill her?"

Noah pushed open the archive room door before turning to her. "Because he didn't."

Chapter 16

After Noah dropped that bomb, Claire followed him in silence for a moment. "What do you mean, he didn't? He didn't kill her?" She shook her head in astonishment. "Then why are we even here?" Claire felt defeated. If Hank didn't kill his first wife, she had no leverage to get Faith out of marrying him. She barely noticed Noah pulling out a chair for her, but she sat in it with an exaggerated sigh.

He pulled an archive off the shelf and placed it in front of her. "We're here to find proof that he killed his second wife."

Claire's eyes widened at that bit of news. "He was married twice before?"

Noah nodded as he opened the archive to the end of October 1929. Claire read a few headlines before she realized the articles discussed Black Tuesday, the stock market crash that started the Great Depression. Noah pointed to one of the articles. "Hank got cocky…thought he could trade on the margins. He lost everything, and Tina was a few weeks from delivering their child."

Claire didn't know her eyes could get any bigger, but she stared at Noah with her mouth agape. "She was pregnant?"

"There were complications. Neither she nor the baby made it." Noah flipped a few more pages to Tina's obituary on November 5th.

Claire read the old newsprint in shock. "He truly did lose everything," she remarked with a hint of sadness. If she didn't know what he had planned for Noah and Faith, she might have felt sympathy for him. He had been married, widowed and broke by the age of nineteen. What had all that done to a teenager? Claire took a deep breath. She knew what it had done. It had turned him into a murderer. "And you don't think he had anything to do with Tina's complications in birth?"

Noah groaned softly. "That's all I've done for weeks, but there just isn't any proof of foul play. All their friends and colleagues felt confident that Hank loved Tina and looked forward to being a father. He seemed to dote on her. Complications arose a few weeks before she gave birth, and her doctor put her on bed rest…nothing out of the ordinary." Noah sat beside Claire and ran his fingers through his tousled hair. "Hank comes from money, you know? His parents died when he was eighteen and left him everything. Unfortunately, he put it all in the stock market including all the money he got from marrying Tina. He kept hoping it would recover, and it did for a while, but then it got hit again in 1932. What little he had managed to recover was then lost forever. I saw Hank shortly after that, and I swear I didn't recognize him. I thought then that it was losing Tina and the baby, but now I'm not so sure." He grabbed several archives and placed them on the table in front of Claire, "and things aren't as clear with Meredith." Claire looked at the dates in the new archives.

"Meredith?" She asked without looking up. All the archives had the same year on them. "He got married again in 1932?"

Noah nodded with a shrug as he slid one of the archives closer to her. "I wasn't invited to that wedding and didn't even know about it." He stopped with a groan, again running his hands through his hair. "I had just assumed he meant Tina."

His comments confused Claire. "What do you mean? Who did you think meant Tina?"

Noah groaned again, biting his lip as he turned to Claire. "When Mr. Baltimore hired me to find out what happened to his daughter, I assumed he meant Tina…not Meredith. I didn't know Hank had a second wife, though in hindsight it was obvious."

Though still confused, Claire nodded. "You mean you didn't know about Meredith?"

"When I was hired, he never mentioned her name. Mr. Baltimore must have assumed I knew whom he was talking about. I just found out about Meredith." He paused with a frown. "That's what that note was that Nancy brought to me while you were in the office. It asked me if there was an update on Meredith. I made a few phone calls to verify who she was, so I haven't even had time to do much research yet. I was hoping you would help, especially after what happened last night?" He asked her with an apologetic smile.

Claire's eyes widened before she nodded frantically, grabbing for the large book in front of her. "Damn right! Anything that will help me nail that bastard to the cross."

She missed Noah's surprised look as she opened the archive and looked at the front page of the newspaper from July 1st, 1932. "Mr. Baltimore didn't give you the date of his daughter's wedding? And I thought you knew Tina? Didn't you know her last name wasn't Baltimore?"

Noah sat in the chair across the table from her and grabbed another archive. He shook his head with a sigh, "I had met Tina a few times, but I honestly can't recall ever hearing her last name. All Mr. Baltimore did was hand me an envelope full of cash and told me to find out what happened to his daughter. Apparently, he's tried numerous investigators but none of them could get close enough to Hank. He approached me since he knew we were friends." He paused to give Claire a sheepish look. "I don't really do this as a career. It was mostly a favor…and it was a lot of money. I sound so inept about all this, but in reality, I don't really have much experience with this kind of thing…or I might have verified the daughter's name, and the date of the wedding. I had stars in my eyes." He chuckled softly. "I've never had anyone throw so much money at me before."

Claire smiled softly at his endearing honesty. She had to clasp her hands in her lap to keep from reaching out to him. "You don't come from money as well?"

Noah smiled as he turned a page of the archive in front of him. "My parents' money is not mine. This was money I would earn for myself. That has always meant more to me. I've always felt I should pay my own way."

"I know what you mean," she muttered. Claire had felt that way after her accident. She wanted to get independent and not rely on her parents' generosity, even though she knew they would have willingly taken care of her for the rest of her life. Claire hadn't wanted that. She had wanted to make her own money and take care of herself. A smile touched her lips as she realized she had finally been succeeding in that endeavor, when she was thrust back to 1935. It hadn't even been a week since she had been in her own time, but it felt like a lifetime. Claire wondered how she would ever fit in back there again. Needing to change the line of her own thoughts, she forced her mind back to the conversation. "Do you have any idea of when the marriage took place?"

Noah sighed again before continuing. "All I really know is that Hank wasn't married when I saw him in July, so we'll just need to go through the rest of the year until we find something."

It didn't take very long for Claire to get to the aforementioned stock market crash, since it happened on July 8th. The article quoted that the stock market hadn't been as low since the 1800's. Claire read with a bit of surprise, since she had only thought the market had crashed in 1929. It was no wonder the economy hadn't recovered for so long, if two such huge crashes happened a few years apart from each other. Hank had lost what little he had managed to recover. Claire shook her head to think that while some people had resorted to killing themselves over the loss, Hank had turned to killing others. She flipped the page and continued searching.

Claire's eyes began to cross, when she finally stumbled upon a grainy black and white photo of a wedding party. She gasped, "I think I've found something."

She had started on a second archive from 1932 and hadn't even noticed the date. She slid the opened book toward Noah, who looked with widened eyes.

"September, huh? This isn't even the same man I saw a few months earlier. He had been at the end of his rope, but he's smiling here as if on top of the world."

Claire looked at the picture again and grimaced. He had the same smiling leer that had been in Faith's wedding picture. She knew as soon as she saw it that he had already planned his next wife's death. "Meredith was rich, wasn't she?" She asked softly.

Noah shrugged. "I doubt he would have married her otherwise, and Mr. Baltimore is very generous with his checkbook." He scanned the article and nodded. "Oh yes, she came from a very wealthy family. Apparently, Mr. Baltimore is an oil tycoon." He chuckled. "Guess that's why he hired me."

Claire slid her chair around the table so that she could sit beside Noah. "I just can't imagine why she married him. So now we need to look for her obituary?"

Noah nodded with a grim expression and began to flip pages. Claire figured she should look through the last archive, just in case the murder hadn't happened shortly after the wedding. When Noah announced he had found it, she breathed a sigh of relief and looked at the article in front of him, noting the date.

"Two months later? You would think all fingers would have pointed to Hank."

Noah nodded as he read the rest of the article. "According to this, he was out of the state when she died."

"How did it happen?"

Noah read a bit more. "Says she drove her car off a cliff."

"What?"

Noah nodded and flipped a few more pages. "So he actually waited two months to kill her, but he got away with it." She muttered under her breath. "How did he manage killing her while he was out of state?"

"I guess he planned it well." Claire shook her head as she absorbed all he had told her. "Wait a minute. I'm confused. When I was at Hank's house Sunday, you told me that he was able to afford it because of Tina."

Noah sighed with a smile. "A lot has changed since then. I didn't know that he got his money from Meredith and not Tina. Though I probably shouldn't even have said as much as I did that day, but I felt close to you for some reason." He paused to stare into her eyes. "It is strange how I feel like I've known you for years, and do you realize how uncommonly bright you are for a teenager? I keep forgetting that you're not my age." He finished with a chuckle.

Claire momentarily forgot about what they had been discussing. "I feel the same way." She felt herself being drawn closer to him, and she stared at his lips. His comment about her intelligence then sunk in and ruined the moment. She nodded and leaned back.

Noah cleared his throat. "So, how do you think Hank managed to kill Meredith while he was out of the state?"

She blinked a few times before his question registered in her flustered brain. "Well, I doubt security is that strong now. He might have used another name and snuck back home, or maybe he never left at all and only made it look like he did."

Noah looked confused. "What do you mean by security isn't that strong now? As opposed to what?"

Claire winced with a sigh. "I don't know what I mean. I'm just confused."

He frowned at her evasiveness before shaking his head. "Says here he was working for her father and was on a business trip. Has witnesses putting him there."

"Maybe he paid them off…Or maybe he messed with the brakes of the car, so that it would take a few days for them to give out, which would give him enough time to make sure he wasn't around."

Noah stared into her eyes for a moment before he looked back at the article. "The car incinerated, so there wasn't much for them to investigate."

Claire licked her lips. "Well, this should be enough for the Pruitts to rethink this marriage." She looked around the basement.

"That's what you call your parents?" Noah asked softly.

She didn't hear the question at first as another thought wormed its way into her brain. "If he got rich off Meredith's death, what is he getting out of marrying Faith?" Her voice was barely above a whisper but then Noah's quiet comment finally sunk in. She thought at first she should ignore it as she continued to look around the room.

"What are you looking for?"

"A copy machine?" She suddenly gasped and made eye contact with Noah. "Do they have those now?"

Noah stood and gently grasped her shoulders. "There's that now talk again, and don't tell me you're just confused. Something's going on here, and I'd like to know what it is. You call your parents by their last name and now refer to yourself in the third person? What is going on, Faith?"

She bit her lip and stared into his expressive eyes. She so badly wanted to reveal everything to him. "I wish I could tell you." Claire responded, lifting a hand to his chest.

Being so absorbed in Noah, the gasp didn't get her attention right away. Noah frowned and turned his head. His widened eyes made Claire turn her head to look. When her gaze locked onto another set of shocked eyes, she cringed.

"Oh, damn," she muttered.

Chapter 17

Hector Pruitt stared back at Claire with a mixed expression of surprise and outrage. His gaze slowly moved to Noah before returning to his daughter's face.

"Faith," Hector nearly whispered as he approached them.

Claire didn't know what to do. She couldn't run away and hide, but she had no idea what to say to Hector. She licked her suddenly dry lips.

"Father, what are you doing here?"

He made a choked sound that ended in a gasp. "What am I doing here? Shouldn't that be the other way around, young lady? Didn't you tell your mother you were going to school with Janet?" He turned a scrutinizing eye to Noah, "and what are you doing here with my daughter, young man? Does Hank know she's with you?"

Claire looked up at Noah to see him shake his head. "No sir, I –"

"How did you know I was here?" She interrupted him, turning back to Faith's father.

Hector shook his head and grabbed her upper arm. "Let's go home, Faith." He tried to lead her to the door, but she held her ground.

"No, wait!" She nearly yelled, looking back to Noah. He shrugged, clearly at a loss of what he could do to help her.

Hector pulled her close to him and hissed in her ear. "Don't make me turn you over my knee. You are not too old for a good lashing."

Tears filled her eyes as her brain tried to comprehend what he had just threatened her with. Would he actually spank her in a public library…in front of Noah?

"Say goodbye to Noah, my dear. I need to get you home. You have a wedding to get ready for."

Her throat constricted as air fought its way into her lungs. Claire shook her head. "But wait. You have to see what we've found." She pointed at the opened archive. "Hank was married twice. Did you know that? Both of his wives died."

Hector barely spared a glance at the table before lifting his gaze to Noah. "I think you should have a talk with Hank before you show up at the wedding tomorrow, Noah. He might not want you there anymore!"

With that he turned and walked away, dragging a shaking Claire behind him. When the door closed behind them, she repeated her earlier question. "How did you know I was here?"

At first it looked like he had no intention of telling her, but then he sighed. "Janet called me."

"She what?" Claire asked in shock, totally confused. "Why did she do that?"

Hector stared into her face for a moment. "Janet was in tears when she called. She said she was worried about you and followed you when you left the school. She saw you get into Noah's car." He shook his head, the disappointed expression deepening across his face.

Even though he wasn't her father, that look tore at her heart. "But don't you even care that both of Hank's wives died?"

Hector didn't look her way as they climbed the stairs out of the basement. "Are you really trying to convince me that you're here to dig up a reason to stop the wedding? It won't work, Faith." He gestured behind them. "I saw the two of you when I walked in there. You weren't researching. You were practically in his arms. First Janet and now this man? Have you no pride?"

Claire gasped. "I haven't done anything wrong! Not with Janet and not with Noah. I'm trying to get you to understand that Hank isn't who you think he is. The man's a monster."

Hector tightened his grip on her arm, making her wince. "I want no more of such talk. That man will be your husband in less than a day, so you will show him some respect."

"I'll die first," she threatened.

Her voice carried a bit as they entered the main library. Hector sucked in his breath, as a few of the patrons looked their way. He forced a smile and walked faster, not saying another word until they stepped outside.

"You're acting like a child, Faith, and I won't stand for it! What is going on in that head of yours? You're acting and talking crazy."

They stopped at Hector's car, and he opened the passenger door for her. She stared up at him with pleading eyes. "Please, Father, don't make me marry him." Not knowing what else to say, she panicked. "I'll run away."

She winced as she realized she had said the wrong thing. Hector's face clouded over.

"We'll see about that." He nearly shoved her into the car and slammed the door, quickly going around to the driver's side. Claire contemplated opening the door and running off, but she delayed too long. Hector got in and started the car, pulling away from the library. Claire looked out the window just in time to see Noah watching them drive off, a look of consternation on his face. He mouthed, "I'm sorry." She bit her lip to keep from waving to him, but she watched him until they turned a corner, blocking him from her view. Tears filled her eyes, and she took a deep breath. "What am I going to do now?" Claire muttered under her breath.

"What was that?" Hector asked.

She looked at him and clenched her jaws. "Nothing." Claire had never felt so lost. How had things gotten so messed up?

They arrived at the house a few minutes later, and Hector gripped her arm for the walk inside. Claire wondered if he would tie her up and gag her until morning. Margie appeared from the kitchen and looked at them in surprise.

"What's going on? Hector? Faith?"

"I'll tell you when I come back down." Hector told his wife as he led Claire toward the staircase and then upstairs.

Claire frowned and tried to joke with him. "Isn't a dungeon usually in the basement?"

He didn't respond but merely pursed his lips together. "I'm going to let you contemplate your actions of late. I'll have your mother bring you something to eat later, but you aren't to leave your room."

Claire's eyes widened upon hearing that. "Until when?"

They stopped outside Faith's bedroom door, where Hector faced Claire. "Until your wedding."

She shook her head, "but that's tomorrow! I have to stay in my room until then?" She suddenly wished she hadn't delayed jumping out of the car at the library. She would now be a prisoner until her forced marriage to Hank. Claire shook her head harder, "but you can't do this," she moaned, very near tears.

Hector looked at her with something akin to sympathy in his gaze. "My darling daughter, you are still a minor and my child. I can do what I want, and when you are safely married to Hank, he will then take over and do what he wants." He stepped closer and grasped both of her arms. "You just don't understand the shame you could bring upon this family, Faith. You *will* be a married woman in the morning. Maybe that will straighten things out in your head."

With that he opened the door and gestured toward the room. "In you go."

Not wanting to see if he would actually shove her inside, Claire nodded and entered the room. She turned to look at Faith's father, but he closed the door in her face. She stood there for a moment wondering if he would lock her in, but she didn't hear anything. After waiting a few minutes, Claire tried the door. It opened, and she slowly pushed it further, cringing at the loud creak.

Hector appeared in the doorway, and she jumped back with a shriek. He shook his head and slammed the door shut. This time she heard the key sliding in and the resounding click of the lock. "Oh, damn," she muttered, placing her forehead against the heavy wooden door.

Pushing herself away from the door, Claire stepped back until she came up against the foot of the bed. She slid down to the floor and buried her face in her hands. Horrible thoughts began to flood through her mind. What if the wedding went ahead as planned, and it didn't matter that she said no? What if the preacher would endorse the wedding, even if she didn't want it? He might be on the Pruitts' side. What if she failed in her mission to stop the wedding? She knew that if Hank got his hands on her, he would kill her. Claire lifted her head and caught Faith's reflection in the mirror.

Finally, she wondered if she asked him, would Noah run away with her? If they both went far enough, maybe Hank wouldn't be able to find them, and if he couldn't find them, he couldn't kill them. Tears trickled down Faith's cheeks as Claire shook her head. She looked at the door again, realizing she couldn't escape that way. Her gaze went toward the window, already knowing that jumping would at least break her legs if not her neck. She closed her eyes and laid her head against the footboard, as she fantasized about Noah following them from the library and pulling Claire out of Hector's clutches. They could have run off together and lived happily ever after. If they had, she wouldn't be locked in Faith's room to await her doom.

She didn't know how much time passed before the door unlocked, and Margie walked in carrying a tray. The older woman had obviously been crying as she placed the tray on the desk before facing Claire.

"Get up off the floor, girl, before you catch cold."

Claire shook her head. "You can't catch a cold that way."

Margie's eyes widened at such a response, but she ignored it with a sigh. "I must say I am quite chagrined with you. I actually believed you this morning, when you said you wanted to go to school. To find out that you actually lied to me?" She blinked a few times before shaking her head, "and then to find out you were in a dark library basement with Hank's best man? I'm…I'm just so shocked… and appalled."

Claire's eyes had dried a long time before, so she just returned Margie's stare. She was at wit's end and didn't know how much longer she could pretend to be this woman's daughter. The tears may have dried up, but she still felt the hurt of realizing that she and Noah could not run off together. Claire did not belong in this time or in this body. She didn't belong with Noah either, but that didn't stop it from hurting. "He's a good kisser, too. Much better than Hank…or Janet for that matter."

Margie gasped as her mouth fell open. "What?" She whispered.

Claire nodded. "Yeah, it is just too bad it's not Noah you're forcing me to marry. Now there's a man I'd like to see naked."

Margie placed a hand to her chest and stepped back. "You and he…you two haven't… have you?"

"Do you mean have I fucked him? No, not yet!" Claire glared at her, wanting to hurt her, not caring what happened at that moment. In her mind they could do nothing worse than they were already doing.

"Watch your mouth, young lady, or I'll take the soap to you!"

Claire pushed herself to her feet and took a step toward Margie. "Try it!" She challenged as lightning bolts of anger flashed across her eyes.

Margie suddenly looked frightened and shook her head. "You're not my daughter. What have you done to my Faith?"

"You killed her!" She yelled. "By making her marry that man," Claire finished just above a whisper, feeling guilty as soon as she said it. Margie's face nearly crumbled.

"I just want my daughter back. Your father can't abide your relationship with Janet. It would destroy his reputation and his standing in the community and his company. Can't you understand that? Why do you have to hurt me like this? I love you, Faith. I hope you believe that." As if not able to be in the same room with her any longer, Margie turned and fled the room.

Claire ran across the room and tried to open the door, but Margie had locked it behind her. Claire beat it with her fists. "You can't keep me locked up in here…please!"

"I'm sorry, Faith. Please understand this is for the best. We'll let you out in the morning." Margie's muffled voice came through the thick wood.

"Damn it!" Claire muttered and banged her forehead against the door. "Damn!" She turned her back to it and stared at the room, wishing for a way out. As her gaze went to the closet, her eyes widened. "Oh, my God!"

Claire flew across the room and pulled the closet door open, going to the back and tapping on the wall. She felt so stupid right then and wondered how she could have forgotten about the secret entrance to the attic.

Chapter 18

After she got the door open to reveal the staircase, Claire stuck her head out of the closet. She half expected to see Margie and Hector framed in the doorway, but they weren't there. The door remained shut and most likely still locked. Claire gnawed on her lower lip as she again faced the staircase. Her gaze went from the bottom step to the top one. She wondered if the stairs would creak? That would certainly remind the Pruitts that they had left her in a room with access to the attic.

Knowing she couldn't just stand there, Claire took a deep breath and stepped forward. She climbed one step and then another. So far so good, so she continued to climb the stairs. When she reached the top step, Claire realized she had been holding her breath and let it out in a whoosh. She looked over her shoulder to stare at her closet door and swallowed the lump in her throat.

"You can do this, Claire," she whispered to herself and turned to emerge into the attic. Her gaze swept across the dusty room. Many of the same things she had seen on her previous visit still sat in the same places, though there weren't nearly as many boxes. Remembering the portrait, Claire's gaze flew to the window. She sighed at not seeing the wrapped frame leaning there and turned to look for it elsewhere. After five minutes of searching, she surmised that it must have been stored somewhere else. "Damn," she cursed silently.

Not wanting to waste any more time in the attic, Claire turned toward the dumbwaiter and slid the door open. She hoped it would be at the attic, but no such luck. Claire stuck her head in and stared down, but she couldn't see more than one floor through the darkness below. She looked for the controls and then groaned softly as she noticed that it hadn't been electric in 1935. Looking up, she saw a pulley with rope looped around it, the two ends hanging down and then disappearing into the abyss below. Claire realized she would have to bring the dumbwaiter to the attic herself. She licked her dry lips, wondering how loud that would be. Taking a deep breath, she grabbed one end of the rope and began to pull.

Sweat dripped down her face by the time the little elevator appeared in front of her. Luckily, it hadn't made that much noise on its ascent, so Claire doubted the Pruitts had heard anything. She still snuck a look behind her to make sure they didn't emerge from the stairs.

Looking back at the dumbwaiter, Claire studied how it worked. Before, she had just slid in and then pushed a button. After some searching, she found the break and applied it. She certainly didn't want it careening back down while she attempted to get inside. Claire climbed in and then took a deep breath, grabbing the rope that fed its way through the top and then bottom of the elevator. When she had a firm grip, she released the break. Not expecting the freefall, Claire had to choke back a scream and grabbed for the rope with both hands. It felt like her hand went up in flames as the rope burned her palm, but she knew she couldn't let it go. Once she finally got it to stop, she held her breath and listened, half expecting to hear the Pruitts shouting. When she only heard the sound of her own heart beat, she used both hands to slowly bring the dumbwaiter down through the bowels of the house. Ignoring the pain in her hand, she counted the doors as she passed them, being extra quiet as she passed the first floor. Claire had not seen the Pruitts using the dumbwaiter since she had been there, so she could only hope they didn't choose that moment to start.

When she reached the basement, she let out a deep breath and sighed. Claire slid the door open slowly, just in case someone might be in the basement. Her luck still held as she looked into the empty room. She slid out of the dumbwaiter and something caught her eye. Upon giving it her full attention, she discovered the wrapped portrait. Claire raced over to it and ripped the paper off the front, revealing Faith's face but her own expression.

She could only stare at the portrait at first, relieved that it hadn't been taken out of the house. Claire had feared she would never see it again, and she somehow knew that she could never go home without it. She held out a shaking hand, fully intending on touching Faith, but something stopped her. Claire's gaze went from her hand, less than an inch from the portrait, to Faith's face. She then shook her head, knowing she couldn't leave yet. She hadn't stopped Hank, and she hadn't stopped the wedding. Claire ignored the voice telling her that she also couldn't leave without seeing Noah one last time.

Her hand began to throb, and she held up her open palm to look at it. Claire winced to see the bloody scrapes and looked around the basement for something to wrap her hand in. Finding a rag, she ripped it and then tied it around the wound. She then looked around the basement, her gaze resting on the small window near the ceiling. When the room had been set up as her darkroom, she had painted that window black, but now its clear glass revealed the darkness beyond. Claire looked around for something to climb on, since she knew she wouldn't be able to use the basement stairs and leave by the front door. She found a stool and moved it beneath the window. Using a broom handle, she managed to get the window open. Claire looked back at the portrait and wished she hadn't ripped the paper it had been wrapped in. She wouldn't let the portrait out of her sight, but she didn't want to take the chance of it getting damaged…or take the chance of touching it before she wanted to. She found an old tarp and wrapped it around the portrait, before tying it up with twine. Claire grabbed her bundle and then climbed up on the stool, pushing the wrapped portrait out the basement window. She then pulled herself up and through it, landing on the grass outside.

Claire closed the window behind her and crouched against the house, her back leaning against the cool concrete. She had no idea of the time as she stared up at the moon. Luckily, it wasn't full, which would illuminate the yard, increasing the chances of her being seen. She closed her eyes and took a deep breath. As hard as it had been getting out of the house, she still needed to make her way across town and find Noah's office. Claire had no guarantee that he would even be there, but she had nowhere else to go. If she had to, she would camp out in the bushes until he showed up.

Taking another deep breath and tightening her grip on the portrait, Claire sprinted away from the house toward the nearest tree. She stayed to the shadows until she felt certain she couldn't be seen by anyone inside the house. When she had gone a block, she slowed her pace and sighed, though she kept looking over her shoulder. She hid every time she heard a car, afraid that it would be Hector coming after her.

Claire hadn't gone even a mile when the portrait felt as if it weighed over a hundred pounds. She shifted it to her other arm, before finally settling it on her head and holding it with both hands.

By the time she reached downtown, she thought she would die from sheer exhaustion. In her opinion walking was definitely overrated. Claire almost chuckled out loud, realizing how hypocritical she sounded. She would have given anything to be able to walk freely in her own body, and she actually complained about being able to in another. After making sure that no cars came, Claire sat on a nearby bench and placed the portrait on the ground at her feet. She tried to remind herself she'd had it worse. Those years of painful rehab had nearly done her in, but she had made it through. Faith's young and healthy body could withstand a little more abuse.

Nodding, Claire stood and grabbed the portrait. She only had a few more blocks to go before she reached Noah's office, and then she could relax. She doubted Hector knew anything about that. No one would find her there.

A few minutes later Claire stood outside the office, sweat dripping down her face. She could also feel it dripping down her back and between her breasts. She realized she must look a fright and felt sort of relieved that Noah wouldn't see her in such a state. Claire watched in shock and surprise as the door of the office opened and Noah stepped out. He started upon seeing her.

"Faith?"

He stared at her as if she were a ghost.

"Noah? You're here?"

He nodded, coming forward to take the portrait out of her arms. "You look like death. Did you walk here?"

She almost didn't let him take the portrait, but she was too tired. "You're here?" She repeated dumbly before everything went dark.

Claire opened her eyes to see Noah staring down at her. Concern flooded his handsome features as he wrung a towel in a bowl of water before placing the damp cloth on her forehead.

"Damn, did I pass out?" She asked with a bit of disgust. That had been the second time she fainted in front of him. Claire blushed at such a girly thing to do. She had certainly never done that in her own body.

"Here, drink this." He held a glass of water to her lips, and she watched him as she swallowed some of it. Her dry throat made it painful to swallow, but she forced herself to drink some more.

"I didn't think you would be here, but I had no where else to go." Claire said.

Noah nodded. "I didn't know if I should go to Hank's or not. If your father called and told him about us being at the library, I didn't want a confrontation." He gestured to the portrait. "What is that and why did you carry it here?"

Claire didn't break eye contact with him as she shrugged. "It's a portrait of…of me. It's important that it stays with me."

Noah frowned. "Why? What happened after Hector took you home, Faith?"

"Nothing. He just locked me in my room."

Noah smiled, "and you escaped?"

Claire sat up and winced at the painful throbbing in her hand. "I guess you can say that."

Noah followed her gaze to her wrapped hand. "What happened?" He asked as he removed the torn rag from her palm, wincing as it pulled away from her skin. She sucked the air through her clenched teeth.

"Casualties of war, I guess," she tried to joke but couldn't muster up even a small smile.

"I need to clean this, or it could get infected."

Claire watched Noah move around the office, bringing back his first aid kit. She could only stare at him as he cleaned and bandaged her hand. Claire pulled her lip between her teeth as she fought the desire to run her other hand through his thick hair.

"I don't know what to do next, Noah. The wedding is supposed to take place tomorrow. The Pruitts will discover that I'm gone. They'll tell Hank, and I suppose they will all look for me. Is there the slightest chance that any of them know about this place?"

Noah looked up at her. "No, but we can't stay here forever, and I still have a job to do. True, it won't be as easy once Hank discovers I'm working against him, but I still have to do it."

"But you won't be able to finish your job, Noah. Hank will kill you. When he finds out about you, he will want us both dead."

Noah sighed and sat on the edge of the couch. "Well, I would like to think I'm smarter than Hank."

Claire touched his arm. "Oh, I'm sure you're smarter, but I think he's more cunning…and evil." Her lower lip trembled. "I don't want anything to happen to you. Can't we just leave?"

Noah licked his lips before meeting her gaze. "I can't just take off. I'm not a coward, Faith. If I have to face Hank to get this sorted out, then I guess that's what I'll do."

She gripped his sleeve in her fist and inched closer to him. "Self preservation is not cowardice. Noah, you don't seem to realize what he's capable of. So far he's only killed women, but…" Her voice trailed off as tears filled her eyes. Claire shook her head and moved her hand to his face, her index finger lightly tracing his lower lip.

He shifted his body to face her and gently gripped her arms. "Nothing is going to happen to me, Faith. You have my word on that."

Claire smiled, moving her other hand to his chest. "Can I get that in writing?"

Noah studied her face for a moment, moving one of his own hands to caress her cheek, his thumb moving lightly across her mouth. She parted her lips and licked the pad of his thumb. Noah watched her tongue and sighed. When she sucked his finger into her mouth, he gasped.

"Faith?"

"Hmmm?" She responded, suckling the thumb in her mouth.

He opened his mouth to speak, but only a groan came out. Noah pulled his hand away from her face and replaced it with his mouth. Claire moaned in response as she wrapped her arms around him to deepen the passionate embrace.

Chapter 19

As soon as their lips met, Claire was lost. She had seen movies and read romance novels and had scoffed at the idea of a simple kiss driving a woman wild, but every one of Noah's kisses proved her wrong. It simply amazed her how good he felt and tasted. She pulled his tongue even farther into her mouth as she stroked it with her own. Noah moaned deep within his throat and tightened his grip on her, kneading her back through her shirt.

His lips trailed kisses down her throat, and her head fell back as he licked her flesh. She slid both of her hands into his hair, pressing his face even closer to her. When she felt his hot mouth on her naked breast, Claire gasped. She hadn't even realized he had unfastened her shirt. Glancing down to watch him suckle her sent quivers down her back, and she bit down on her lower lip.

Claire knew that no one would interrupt them, and she had a momentary doubt. Should she let it continue? She dealt with Faith's body, not her own, and she didn't know if she had the right to give away the girl's innocence. Noah must have sensed her indecision and looked up at her.

"Maybe we shouldn't be doing this."

She looked into his passion filled gaze and sighed. Tears misted her eyes as she realized she couldn't stop him...didn't want to stop him. She needed him more than air.

"I can't imagine anything else we should be doing," she whispered and reclaimed his mouth. He pulled her up against his body as she straddled him, wrapping her ankles behind his back. When she felt his erection between her legs, Claire smiled. "God, you feel good," she breathed against his mouth. Wanting to feel his flesh and not his shirt, she began to undo the buttons. Noah looked down to watch for a moment before meeting her gaze.

"So do you." Noah moaned, and Claire pushed the shirt down his shoulders, kissing the exposed skin. Noah shrugged out of the shirt, letting it fall to the floor beside them before sliding a hand up one of her exposed thighs. Claire sighed as his hand crept between her legs and pushed her panties aside. Her eyes widened with a groan as she felt him slip a finger inside of her.

"Damn, you're so wet. How can you be so wet?" He asked with a gasp.

Claire didn't know how to respond to that, kissing him deeply instead. She caressed his chest with her fingertips, tracing the taut muscles of his abdomen. Gaining courage from his actions, she slid a hand between them and placed it on his crotch. Her mouth fell open slightly to feel the size of him through his slacks. "Oh my! I think it's a good thing that I'm so wet." He felt huge.

He groaned at her comment, tightening his free arm around her. "Will this be your first time, Faith?"

Claire closed her eyes, hating for him to call her that while they were being intimate. She shook her head, wanting so badly to tell him her real name. She reached for his zipper and slowly tugged it downward. So intent on her task, she didn't at first realize he had stopped moving. Claire focused on his face. "What?"

"You've been with someone else?"

It took a moment for the question to penetrate her fogged brain, but then she shook her head. "Oh, God no! Are you kidding? Remember, I'm a lesbian." Claire almost laughed at his expression. "Well, at least I was until I met you." She licked her lips and smiled at him, sliding a hand into his slacks to stroke his erection. Mustering up more courage, she wrapped her fingers around his girth, and Noah's eyes widened. He shifted, reminding her of his finger within her. He moved another finger inside as his thumb began to stroke the little nub of sensitive flesh nearby. Claire gasped at the sensation, tightening her hold on his engorged flesh. She licked her lips and stared into his expressive eyes, before running her hand up and then back down his shaft.

"Oh, my God!" Noah groaned. "I want to be inside you. This is killing me." He kissed her deeply, before holding her close to whisper in her ear. "That's all I've been able to think about since I first kissed you."

"Me, too," she breathed into his ear. "I love you, Noah." She wasn't sure if she should say it, but nothing had ever felt more right to her.

She felt him smile against her cheek before he tightened his arm around her. "I love you too, Faith."

"Call me Claire." She nearly begged.

"What?" Noah asked, pulling back slightly to look into her face, his hand moving from within her. Claire pulled his erection free of his slacks and positioned it at the opening to her body. She didn't want to move to take off her underwear, so she just slid it aside. Pulling up slightly, she then slowly brought her weight down onto him, never breaking eye contact.

"I want you to call me Claire." She winced as her body stretched to accommodate his size, but she refused to close her eyes. She kept her gaze locked on Noah, whose mouth fell open with pleasure. He licked his lips before nodding.

"I'll call you whatever you want me to…Claire."

She smiled, loving the sound of him saying her real name. "Tell me you love me." She slid down another inch.

"I love you…Claire."

Tears filled her eyes as she took another inch of him. It hurt more than she expected it to. She doubted that Faith had ever been able to use tampons to help stretch her hymen, as Claire was pretty sure that's what she felt tearing. Her own doctor had assured her that tampon use would keep her first time from hurting as much. Of course, when she had been in the 21st century, she would never have guessed she'd be losing her virginity in

1935, let alone being in someone else's body when she lost it. "Oh, God!"

"Don't cry, Faith…I mean, Claire. Don't cry, baby!" Noah wiped her eyes and then kissed her cheeks before reclaiming her mouth, tightening his arms around her even more. She dug her fingernails into his shoulders as she dropped down a bit more. *How big is he?* She screamed inside her mind.

When she didn't think she could take anymore, Claire finally settled in Noah's lap. She let out the breath she had been holding and leaned against his chest for a moment.

"Are you OK, Claire?" He asked as he stroked her back.

She sighed and nodded, lightly draping her arms around him. "Yeah, I think the worst is over with now."

He chuckled and pulled back to look into her face, caressing her cheeks. "I think you should start to enjoy it now. Lean back against the couch. Let me take over." He undid her shirt the rest of the way and helped her out of it. Her bra followed it to the floor.

Claire wasn't quite ready to move just yet, but she did as he directed. He told her to leave one leg around his waist and to drop her other knee to spread her thighs more. She frowned with an uncertain smile, but then he began to move within her. The first stroke took her by surprise, and she grabbed onto his shoulders.

Noah reached between them to fondle her, licking one of her nipples. She gasped as a jolt of pleasure surged through her body and settled in her pelvis "Is this a favorite pair of panties?" He asked softly.

At that moment, she couldn't have cared less about anything. "Are you kidding?"

"Good!" He smiled and then ripped them off of her.

Claire let out a squeak but then laughed. "I like a man that knows what he wants."

Noah bit his lower lip and nodded, impaling her once again. Claire drew in a shaky breath and let her head fall back against the arm of the couch. While his thumb continued its ministrations on her swollen clitoris, he sped up his thrusts within her. She began to moan as she felt something building up within her. Claire had never masturbated, so she had no idea what an orgasm felt like, and she felt pretty confident that Faith had never had one before either. As Faith's body erupted in its first orgasm, Claire screamed. Noah quickly covered her mouth with his own, muffling the sound as he continued to thrust within her body.

Before the last tremors of the first orgasm subsided, another one exploded within her. Tears filled her eyes and streamed down her cheeks. She dug her nails into Noah's back and shuddered against him. "I can't…I can't…Oh, hell!" She muttered against his mouth.

He suckled her tongue as he sped up his strokes. "Almost…Oh, Claire!" He gave one final thrust and then went still above her, burying his face in her neck. He squeezed her so hard she thought her ribs would crack, but she could only smile through the tears.

Claire wrapped her other leg around his waist and tightened her inner muscles, milking him, loving the feel of him still within her. She could have stayed that way for the rest of her life.

"Damn, I love you!" She mouthed against his cheek.

Chapter 20

Claire stretched with a smile before slowly opening her eyes, finding herself alone on the couch. She had been covered with a light blanket and smiled at the thoughtful gesture. Claire sat up and wrapped the blanket around her shoulders before quickly glancing around Noah's empty office. Wondering where he had gone, she stood, crossed the room and opened the door to peer into the outer office.

She saw him standing in front of Faith's portrait. Claire stood in silence and stared at him, speechless at first. With hands clasped behind his back he leaned forward at the hips to peer at the painting.

"What are you doing?" Claire asked, pursing her lips. She had no idea what would happen should he actually touch the portrait. Fear bubbled up inside her that he might actually be pulled through to another time, and she would never see him again. Claire choked back the laugh at such a ridiculous thought.

Noah looked over his shoulder at her with a full smile, his eyes lighting up when their gazes met. "How are you feeling?" He asked, turning away from the portrait.

Claire approached him, tightening the blanket around her. "Rested…you?" As his gaze traveled down her body, she finally blushed, remembering their intimacy in full detail, not as if the soreness between her legs would have let her forget. She stopped beside him and tore her gaze from his to look at the portrait. "You unwrapped it?"

Noah caressed her back through the blanket as his gaze also returned to the painting. "It is really remarkable, isn't it? Did you know the eyes follow you no matter where you are in the room?"

Claire nodded slowly as she looked back at Noah. "What time is it?" She asked him quietly, glancing around the room for a clock.

"Just past eight." He responded without turning toward her. "I just can't stop looking at it. The artist truly captured you, didn't he? It's almost as if he painted your…your soul."

That got her attention, and she looked back at Faith's face. Had that been what happened? Claire had been there for the actual painting, but then how could she have gone back in the first place if not for the painting? Realizing that she dealt with a paradox, she sighed. What had come first, the chicken or the egg? Claire chuckled but then gasped. Before she could stop him, Noah had reached out and touched a painted cheek. Claire let out a little squeak of protest but then held her breath. He frowned at her reaction as he pulled his hand away.

"Don't worry! I wouldn't hurt it." He sighed, "but you're right. The oils in my hand could damage it. I'm sorry." Noah shook his head. "I just couldn't help it. You call out to me."

"I call out to you?" Claire repeated. She had felt that way about the painting when she first found it. Of course, back then she had thought Faith called to her. Not wanting to look back at the portrait, she looked up at Noah's face instead. She didn't want to risk the need to touch it herself and being pulled into it before she was ready to go. Something within her knew that it wouldn't send her home until she had accomplished what she had been sent to do, and Claire didn't believe she had completed that task yet. She just didn't want to take any chances of being wrong.

Noah nodded his response without looking at her.

"I don't suppose you have a shower here?" She asked hopefully.

He didn't answer at first but then shook his head. "No, but this office suite used to be an apartment, so there is a full bathroom with tub. I'm afraid this little town hasn't advanced enough for showers yet, and I'm a bit surprised you've ever heard of them."

Realizing she had flubbed again, she shrugged. "You'd be amazed what they teach in school nowadays, but of course I meant a bathtub." She finished with a sheepish grin.

He smiled at her. "I've set aside towels for you and even washed your clothes. Let me know if you need anything else. There is also a kitchen here, so I can fix us something to eat while you get cleaned up."

Claire nodded in surprise. "You had time to wash my clothes? How long have you been up?"

"Since six." He paused and looked deep into her eyes. "I've had a lot to think about."

Claire blushed and looked away. "What time does your secretary get here?"

"Not until nine, so you have plenty of time to look presentable…not that you don't look amazing in my blanket." He added with a wink before looking back at the painting. "I'll even rewrap this for you. I have paper and twine, which will be far less cumbersome than that old tarp."

Claire put a hand on his arm and smiled. "Thank you, Noah…for everything."

"Don't mention it." He smiled and caressed her cheek with the back of his hand. "We have much to discuss. We'll have something to eat and then figure out what to do next."

She swallowed the lump in her throat and nodded. "Sounds like a plan. So, where's the bathroom?"

Claire closed the bathroom door and leaned against it. The previous night felt like a dream, but she knew it had been real. She let the blanket fall to the floor at her feet and stared down at Faith's nakedness. Every muscle in her body hurt, but she couldn't stop the smile as it spread across her face.

The mirror above the sink caught her attention, and Claire stared into it. Faith's lips were red and swollen from all those kisses. She let her hands slide down her body and sighed. As she continued to stare at her reflection, the smile melted away. Claire pushed away from the door and approached the sink, never taking her eyes off the mirror.

She grasped the edge of the sink and leaned forward, until only a few inches separated her face from the glass. She stared into Faith's eyes.

"Are you in there, Faith?" Claire whispered. For the first time since she had been in Faith's body, she wondered if the teenager might be in there with her. She had assumed they either switched places or that Faith's mind went somewhere else, but what if she could still see and hear what Claire did? What if she had been there when Noah had made love to her?

She almost gasped at the thought and covered her mouth. "If I've done anything to offend you, I'm sorry," she whispered again. Claire shook her head with a smile, feeling a bit silly talking to her reflection in the mirror. She then realized that she wasn't really talking to herself but to Faith's reflection. Feeling a bit guilty, she looked down at the sink. "I didn't have any right to give away your virginity. I know that, but I want you to know that I love him, and I don't know how much more time I'll have with him. If you're in there, I hope you can forgive me for that. I know I'm supposed to help you, and I really am trying to do that!" Claire looked back up at her reflection to see tears mist her eyes. She let go of the sink and moved to sit on the toilet, looking down at her lap. Her eyes widened to see the traces of dried blood on her upper thighs and gasped as a knock sounded on the door.

"You alright in there?" Noah asked through the wooden frame.

"Yes, I'm fine," she yelled back, wiping her eyes. "I'm about to take that bath." Claire reached over and turned on the water, but she remained seated for a few more minutes. Her gaze fell on her bandaged hand, and she pulled off the gauze to inspect the wound. At least it didn't look infected, but she would be sure to rewrap it after her bath. Claire looked around and noticed the first aid kit on top of her clothes. She smiled at Noah's thoughtfulness, and her mind raced as she thought about the day ahead of her.

Once clean and dry, Claire got dressed. She smiled to see her neatly folded under things, but as she held up the panties she remembered how Noah had ripped them off her. It amused her that he had gone to the trouble of washing them instead of throwing them away. She tossed them into the trash and then slid on her bra. She would just have to go without panties until she could get another pair. Claire frowned, suddenly wishing she had taken the time to pack some clothes before fleeing the Pruitts' home. She certainly couldn't go back, and the only other way she could get clothing would be to rely on Noah's generosity. "Shit," she muttered under her breath, realizing she hadn't thought about any of that and had merely reacted.

Claire sighed and swallowed the lump in her throat. She felt thoroughly unprepared for what was to come, but at least she had Noah in her corner. Claire smiled as she opened a drawer and found his comb. She pulled it out and used it on her hair, before sparing one last glance at her reflection. "Wish us luck," she said with a nod, not entirely sure if she meant her and Noah or her and Faith. "Wish us all luck," Claire quietly added with a sigh.

She found Noah in the kitchen and watched with a smile as he made grilled cheese sandwiches. She approached slowly, enjoying these few moments of him being unaware of her. Noah hummed an unknown song as he flipped the sandwiches. Claire cocked her head to the side, suddenly realizing how quiet it was in the suite. She looked toward the open front window. A cool breeze ruffled the curtain, but no noise came from outside. A contented smile touched her lips at such a peaceful scene. Claire turned back to Noah, to see him staring at her.

"Don't you look like a breath of fresh air," he commented softly.

Claire sucked in her own breath at his sexy tone. She blushed and smiled brightly. "So do you," she responded, walking over to stand by his side. "That smells yummy."

"I hope you like grilled cheese. I don't have many groceries here. I'll shop more later today." He put the sandwiches on a plate. "I'm sure you'll need some more clothes. It looked like the only thing you brought with you was that painting."

Claire nodded. "That was stupid, I know." At his mention of the painting, she turned to gaze around the office until she located it next to Nancy's desk. As promised it had been wrapped in brown paper and tied with twine.

"A bag of clothes might have been lighter as well," he added.

She shook her head. "I couldn't leave the painting behind."

Noah handed her a plate and napkin, before grabbing his own set. He then led the way to the table. "What's so important about that painting, Faith?" Noah frowned as he remembered. "I mean Claire, which reminds me...where did that name come from? I thought your middle name was Mary?"

Claire's eyes widened, since she didn't even know Faith's middle name. She took a seat at the table beside him and shrugged.

Noah sighed deeply and placed his arms on either side of his plate, his sandwich untouched. "Yesterday was a very strange day. You called your parents by their last name, referred to yourself in third person, asked for something called a copy machine, ran away from home with nothing but your portrait, and then you ask me to call you by a totally different name while we were making love." He gazed at her as he said the last part, and she blushed to the roots of her hair.

Claire looked at the sandwich in front of her, to keep from having to meet his searching gaze. "The portrait is just important." She could feel her cheeks getting hot. Noah had noticed so much, and she had no idea how to explain any of it without revealing the truth. He wouldn't be able to accept the truth, so she saw no point in telling him.

Noah sighed. "Obviously, Claire, but I need more than that!" He paused to run his hands through his hair, and she involuntarily licked her lips. She found the man so irresistible that her whole body seemed to vibrate every time she was around him. Claire smiled at her own thought, but his serious expression removed it from her face as soon as it touched her lips.

"Don't you realize what we did last night?" Noah looked at her with a pained expression, but she could only nod. He stared at her a moment. "You were a virgin. I should have known better, but I couldn't stop myself." He groaned softly. "There could have been a gun to my head, and I couldn't have stopped." Noah slammed his hands on the table, startling Claire. He glanced at her and shook his head. "But you're not mine, and I had no right. We might have created life last night." He sighed and looked distractedly across the room.

Claire's eyes widened as his statement sunk in. Pregnancy hadn't even occurred to her. How could she have been so careless with Faith's body? Not only had she given the girl's virginity away, she may very well have gotten her pregnant. She licked her dry lips and shook her head. "Very unlikely that one time would be enough…" Her voice faded as Noah looked at her.

"But not impossible."

"Of course it's not impossible, but so what? I don't regret what happened last night…do you?"

Noah looked stricken. "I can't regret any time I've been with you. I meant it when I said I loved you." He placed both palms on the table and looked thoughtful. When he finally looked at her again, a smile broke out on his gorgeous face. Claire sucked in her breath at the unexpected expression.

"What?" She asked, almost afraid of what he would say.

"You were supposed to get married today, right?"

"Yes," she responded slowly, shaking her head. "I most certainly won't marry Hank, though."

Noah's smile brightened. "No, but would you marry me?"

Chapter 21

Claire's gut instinct told her to blurt out yes, but her rational side stopped her. Had Noah actually just proposed to her? He had no ring and no plans and hadn't even asked on bended knee. Her throat went dry, realizing she had no right to bind Faith to this man, no matter how much she cared for him. Whose name would she sign on the marriage contract? She couldn't sign Claire Todds, and it wouldn't be right to sign for Faith. Claire closed her eyes with a sigh.

"I can't marry you," she whispered. Claire heard movement, and when she opened her eyes, Noah knelt beside her. She sucked in her breath and met his gaze.

"Why not?" He asked softly.

What excuse could she give him? She'd be lying if she said she didn't love him, or that she didn't want to marry him. She wanted to so desperately. She may have known him for less than a week, but she felt as if they had been a part of each other their whole lives. Claire could tell he felt the same way as she reached out to caress his face.

"I'm only seventeen, right? I doubt the Pruitts…I mean my parents…will give their blessing let alone their permission."

Noah frowned, and Claire tried not to cringe. Of course, he had caught her slip at calling Faith's parents by their last name again.

"They might if they find out what happened between us last night." He finally said with a sigh.

Claire gasped. "You wouldn't tell them, would you?"

He shrugged. "What could it hurt, Faith? They want you married, right? I come from the same background as Hank. I'm just as suitable."

Claire frowned. "I don't believe it can be that simple. They have an agreement with Hank and may feel honor bound to see it through. I honestly don't know what would happen if you went to them about wanting to marry me, let alone telling them about last night." She blushed in spite of herself, the memory of their intimacy still so fresh in her mind.

She shook her head. "I also don't want to think of what Hank would do if he realizes you have stolen me away from him." The headline for the deaths of Faith and Noah flashed across her mind. She knew exactly what Hank would do to Noah, so she had to make sure they kept their distance.

"Then we'll just hold out until you turn eighteen. Once you're an adult there won't be anything your parents or Hank can do to stop it."

Claire could feel a headache building. "That's months away…more than half a year." She didn't think she had that much time. She had been sent to 1935 to stop an injustice, not hide out with her lover for seven months or more. Tears threatened to fill her eyes at the notion of staying in Faith's body and marrying the man of her dreams, but nothing about that felt right. She could not steal Faith's life, and she doubted that whatever sent her back would allow her to.

"So what? I have plenty of money. You'll want for nothing, Faith. I want to be with you. Don't you want to be with me?"

His plaintive tone drew her gaze back to his, and she sucked in a shaky breath. "Of course, I feel the same way," Claire responded as tears misted the corners of her eyes. She shook her head, trying to ward them off. "I would love to be with you, but it would have to be as me…not someone else." He would always think of her as Faith first. She would never be Claire to him. She impulsively reached for him and wrapped her arms around him. His strong arms clasped tightly behind her back as he returned the embrace. "But that's impossible," she finished just above a whisper.

Noah shook his head. "What are you talking about? How is it impossible? You're with me now. We can just leave and never come back here."

Claire realized that could be the answer. It could save them both, but what would stop Hank from hunting them down? As long as he lived, they would be in danger…and so would all his future wives.

She then realized what she had been sent back to do, and she tightened her grip on Noah. Claire knew that Hank Holmes had to die. "No, we can't allow Hank to go free. Running won't stop him. He'll just find someone else to marry and kill…and he'll live long enough to run down a defenseless teenager with his car."

Noah pulled away enough to see her face. "What was that?"

She had whispered the last part, so she wasn't surprised he hadn't heard her. "We have to stop him."

"That's not what you said. It was something about a teenager and his car?"

Claire shook her head. "Hank is a very bad man, Noah. If we don't stop him now, he'll become an even bigger monster."

"What do you mean stop him? Do you mean kill him?"

Claire didn't answer, merely returned his inquisitive stare.

"That's murder, Faith."

"I told you to call me Claire." She reminded him with a small smile.

"It's still murder, *Claire*." He repeated with a slight amount of sarcasm.

She shrugged and tried to swallow the lump stuck in her throat. "Didn't you tell me that you would kill him yourself if he came after me?"

Noah narrowed his eyes. "If he dared attack you, then yes, I would defend you...with my life if need be."

Claire shivered as if someone walked over her grave. "Well, I hope it doesn't come to that."

Noah chuckled mirthlessly. "At least we agree on that."

She tried to return the smile as she pulled away, dropping her arms away from him. "You have a gun, right?"

He shook his head. "I'm an investigator, Claire, not a cop."

"Do you have a shovel?" She asked as the image of the weapon from her dream jumped into her mind. The original murder happened at the resort where Hank and Faith had honeymooned. Hank had used a shovel in her dream, but Claire wondered if he had actually used that as the murder weapon. She shuddered at the thought.

Noah burst out laughing until he realized she was serious. He sobered almost instantly and gripped her arms above the elbows. "You're not planning on burying him too, are you?"

She shook her head but then decided that might not be such a bad idea.

"Faith," he scolded with a slight shake. "I don't like where your thoughts are heading."

Claire sighed deeply, almost reminding him again not to call her Faith but then realizing the futility of it. She *was* Faith to him, after all, and that wouldn't change. "Well, do you have one?"

Noah stared blankly at her for a moment. "You mean a shovel? No, I don't have one, and I'm not going to buy one either."

"Maybe you should buy a gun." She pressed.

Noah sighed deeply and released her arms.

"How old do you have to be to buy a gun?" She continued, hardly noticing he had moved back to his own chair.

"You're not buying a gun, Claire, and neither am I."

She looked up in surprise and smiled. He had called her Claire on his own.

"Yes, I remembered that time." Noah said with a serious expression. "It's hard, you know? Your name is Faith, but you want me to call you something else. I don't understand it, but I'm willing to go along with it. I just wish you'd be upfront with me. I know you are keeping something important to yourself, and I should probably be told about it."

"You'd think I was crazy."

"I already do," he countered with a chuckle.

Claire playfully scowled at him. "I do want to tell you everything, Noah, but it would be a waste of time. You wouldn't believe any of it, so what's the point?"

"Because maybe I can help. Can't you give me the benefit of the doubt?"

She sighed. "Cause we have bigger fish to fry. Is it really safe to stay here? I'd feel better somewhere else…somewhere not connected to anyone involved."

Noah frowned at her subject change. "Bigger fish to fry? Quite an expression there." He paused for a moment. "Alright, we'll play it your way for now. My parents own a cabin about an hour from here. We could go there."

"Are you sure that Hank doesn't know about it?" Claire asked.

"I don't see how he could. He's never been there, and I haven't been in years." Noah assured her, "but I thought you didn't want to run away."

Claire bit her lower lip. "It's not running away. We just need a place where we can collect our thoughts and not worry about Hank barging in. We need a place to figure out what to do next."

Once they both agreed on the cabin, they finished their breakfast in silence. Nancy walked in as they were on their way out. She looked very surprised to see them as her gaze went from Claire to Noah.

"Mr. Palmer, you're never in this early."

Noah nodded and placed a hand on the small of Claire's back, and she tried to hide the quiver that ran through her at his touch. Needing the distraction, she walked over to the desk and grabbed the portrait. Noah gestured toward the door as he answered Nancy. "Yes, well, needed an early start. I'll be out of the office all day and will check in tomorrow for any messages."

Nancy nodded as she watched them walk toward the door. "Yes, sir. It was nice seeing you again, Faith."

"You too, Nancy," she responded, clutching the portrait with both hands.

Claire nervously followed Noah to his car, afraid that Hank would jump out at them. She felt half tempted to hold the wrapped portrait up to shield her face, thinking it might be less noticeable but thought better of it. Noah took it from her as they got to his car and gently placed it in the back seat. She took one last look around before climbing into the front seat.

"We'll stay on back roads until we're safely out of town," Noah told her once he sat beside her. He pulled the car away from the curb, and Claire fought the temptation to scrunch down in the seat. Instead, she shielded her face with her right hand and stared out the windshield.

They had been on the road for about fifteen minutes before Claire broke the tense silence. "I can't believe I didn't grab some extra clothes. I don't even have any panties." She blushed in spite of herself.

Noah turned to her with an apologetic smile. "My folks always leave some clothes behind at the cabin. I'm sure there is something of my mother's that you can wear."

Claire cringed at the idea of using someone else's underwear, but beggars couldn't be choosers. She nodded with a small smile as Noah continued.

"I'll stop at the market on the way to get some supplies. We'll need food and basic necessities." He gave her a sideways glance. "You can check to see if they have any...clothing."

Claire brightened and nodded. A frown replaced the smile as a thought occurred to her.

"It's the fourth of September, right?"

"Something special about the date?" Noah asked with a nod.

She shook her head thoughtfully. Faith and Noah originally died on the tenth of September, which would be in six days. Claire gnawed on her lower lip. Did they have to stay in hiding until the eleventh to change the future? She shook her head, remembering that she had already changed the future by altering the day of the wedding, but then an awful thought occurred to her. She had stopped the wedding from happening early by running away, but September seventh hadn't happened yet. So until they got through Saturday, she hadn't really stopped the wedding...at least unless they killed Hank before then. Claire winced at their options.

"What's wrong, Claire?" Noah asked with concern.

She thought about the question before answering. How could she continue keeping the truth from him? She needed an ally and couldn't figure it all out on her own. She needed his help.

Claire turned toward him and gave him a speculative glance. "If I tell you a story, can you keep an open mind and listen to the whole thing without interrupting?"

Noah frowned with a small smile. "A story? Sure, I could use a good story right about now."

She grinned in return and took a deep breath. "OK!" She responded, letting the breath out slowly. "Now, remember, keep an open mind."

Once Noah nodded, Claire began, "there once was a girl named Claire Todds. She had trouble walking because she was hit by a car when she was sixteen and was in constant pain, but one day she happened to drive by this old house that called out to her..."

Claire continued telling him about her trip to the past and tried not to leave anything out. Noah looked at her occasionally throughout, but he kept his mouth shut. She didn't use names, but she could tell when realization dawned as his eyes widened slightly. He looked over his shoulder at the wrapped portrait in the back seat.

"Is that why you need to keep it with you?" He asked in astonishment.

Claire sucked in her breath, not expecting the question. Could that mean he believed her? She followed his gaze for a moment before looking back at his face. Finally, she shrugged. "It's my ticket home...at least I hope that's how it works."

Noah looked serious for a moment before he began to chuckle. "I had no idea you had such a vivid imagination, Faith. That's a remarkable story. Time travel...like H.G. Wells?"

Claire frowned, at first not recognizing the name. She then remembered hearing of a movie about him and nodded slowly. "Sort of." She bit her lower lip. "It's not a story, Noah. I need you to believe me. That's how I know what Hank has planned. He'll kill us both. I've seen it."

"There it is," Noah said suddenly and pulled off the road, turning into a dusty parking lot. Claire looked out the windshield and saw the small market. She hadn't realized she had talked for so long that they had almost reached the cabin. Noah turned to get out of the car, but Claire grabbed his arm.

"Noah?" She asked, fearing she had revealed too much.

He put his hand over hers and gave it a gentle squeeze. "We need to get those supplies for the cabin. We can discuss this some more once we get there."

Claire pulled her hand back and watched in stunned silence as he closed the door and walked toward the market. She didn't know if she should follow him or not, so she just stayed in the car. Had she made a mistake trusting him with the truth?

Chapter 22

Claire stared at the fire and rubbed her arms. She didn't know why she still felt chilly, since she sat on the floor in front of the fireplace. As she glanced over her shoulder toward the small kitchen, she guessed it might have something to do with the indifference Noah had shown since being told the truth. Sighing, her gaze moved to the wrapped portrait leaning against the far wall. Noah had placed it there, and Claire hadn't felt like going near it.

Looking back at the fire with a sigh, she muttered, "I shouldn't have told him."

"And why is that?" His voice being so close surprised her, and she whipped her head around again. Noah stood only a few feet away and held a steaming mug out toward her.

Claire licked her dry lips and reached for the mug, bringing it to her face to sniff its contents.

"It's hot cocoa." Noah answered her unspoken question. "My mother always made it for us when we stayed here. Always took away the chill."

She nodded and blew softly on the hot liquid before taking a tentative sip. It burned as it went down but settled warmly in her stomach. "It's good. Thank you."

"You're welcome," he responded. "I also found this in my folks' room. It should keep you warm." She felt him drape a shawl around her shoulders before taking a seat in the chair closest to her.

Claire looked back at the fire, tightening the soft fabric around her. "Are you going to start treating me like a kid now?" She asked softly.

She heard Noah's soft sigh. "I should never have stopped treating you that way."

Her head turned back to him as she frowned. "I told you the truth."

Noah appeared uncertain as he unblinkingly returned her stare. Finally he looked down at his own mug of cocoa. "I don't know what to believe, Faith. I know I don't believe in time travel, but you expect me to believe your name is Claire Todds and that you are from the future?"

"You told me that you love me," she reminded him, fighting tears.

He sighed, "but who do I love? Faith or Claire?"

"Me," she said simply, silently damning the mist filling her eyes. "You told me that Faith never even looked at you. She loves Janet, and I love you." Her lips quivered on that last statement, and she pursed her lips to still them.

Noah's eyes widened. "You arrived on Friday, didn't you?"

Claire almost smiled her relief but nodded instead. "I can still remember that first moment I set eyes on you. I saw your picture and felt such a strong connection to you. Didn't even know why, but then I never dreamt I would actually meet you…let alone fall in love with you." She swallowed the lump in her throat. "I think I loved you before I even met you."

Noah slid out of the chair and moved closer to her, but he stopped short of reaching her. "I still remember the smile you gave me that night. You had never looked at me before, let alone smiled at me. It almost looked like you were relieved to see me."

Claire chuckled. "I was. Your face was the one I wanted to see the most."

As if she were the painting that compelled others to touch, Noah slowly reached forward to touch her cheek, "but how can it be possible?"

She shook her head with a shrug. "All I know is that something sent me to that house, so I could find the painting. Faith wanted me to help. She even appeared to her mother in dreams."

Claire paused as she thought of everything that had transpired to get her to touch that painting. Mrs. Pruitt hadn't been the only one to have dreams. She had her own the night she had been sent to the past. Claire wondered if Faith had been responsible for that as well.

"Dreams? What kind of dreams?" Noah asked distractedly, his hand on her face going still.

Claire shrugged again. "I'm not really sure. I was told that Mrs. Pruitt agreed to rent her house after Faith told her to in a dream…and the night I was sent here, I dreamt that Hank killed you and Faith with a shovel on his honeymoon."

"A shovel?" He asked, and Claire could tell he remembered her earlier query about owning one. "I've had a few strange dreams lately as well."

"You have? What about? When?" She asked in a rush.

His hand fell into his lap as he sat in front of her. "The first one was on Friday night. Can't remember much of it, but I know you were in it." Noah paused with a blush, and Claire fought a smile. He cleared his throat and continued. "The other one happened last night, after I saw your painting."

"Last night? After we made love?"

Noah nodded. "You went right to sleep, but I was too wired. I got up and cleaned things up. I noticed your painting and thought I'd rewrap it for you, but once I saw it…well, I couldn't take my eyes off it. I must have stared at it for hours and ended up falling asleep in front of it." He paused as if to sort his thoughts and shook his head. "I dreamt of a woman I had never seen before. She was pretty in an unconventional way, but I thought she was enchanting."

Claire's mouth fell open as he described his dream woman and came to the realization he spoke of her. She bit her lip to keep from interrupting him, as he continued to tell her how this woman kept calling his name. She was crying and seemed lost. He had been confused how she knew his name, since he had never seen her before.

"You don't know her name?" Claire asked softly.

Noah focused on her face and then shook his head. "No, but I feel as if I should know it. Strange, huh?"

Claire frowned, wondering why he had dreamt of her crying and calling for him. What could that mean?

"Anyway, I woke up and discovered hours had passed." Noah continued with a sigh. "I checked on you, but you were still asleep, so I finished cleaning up. I washed your clothes and did a few other things around the office, but I kept being drawn back to that painting."

Claire wondered if she should tell him that he had dreamt of her. She ran that question through her mind a few times before slowly shaking her head. He had enough to deal with and didn't need anymore to digest. Chills moved up her arms and then down her back, as she continued to wonder what the dream could have meant.

"What's wrong?" Noah asked with a frown, but she shook her head.

"I don't know. That's just such a strange dream."

He smiled. "Not as strange as trying to believe you are from the future," he reminded her softly.

Claire licked her lips and then chuckled. "Yeah, you got me there."

"Do I?" He asked barely above a whisper, his hand reaching out to touch her. Claire sighed as his fingers made contact with her flesh, the warmth making the chills go away.

She slowly nodded. "Forever."

Their gazes locked and in that instant it didn't matter that he couldn't believe she had come from the future. He loved her, and she loved him. That love was doomed, of course, and Claire tried not to think of that. She stared into his expressive eyes and wanted to stay like that forever, sitting across from him with his hand on her face. It didn't matter what they would do next or what obstacles they would encounter. They had that moment, and it would be with her forever. Claire tried not to cringe as a feeling of foreboding flooded her body, but she tightened the shawl around her.

"I do love you, Noah."

He looked surprised and a bit flustered. "You say that like you're telling me goodbye."

She tried to smile. "Maybe I am." Her gaze involuntarily moved above his shoulder as she focused on the wrapped portrait. Noah had dreamt of her as he slept in front of it. Claire couldn't really be surprised, since the painting was obviously special. It had transported her from the future, after all. "You thought she was enchanting?" The question came out before she could stop it, and her gaze returned to Noah. "I mean the girl from your dream?"

He nodded distractedly. "I've never met anyone quite like her. Her hair was unbound and glorious, sort of like yours is now." He noted and grinned before continuing, his fingers touching

Faith's dark hair. "Yet she wore such strange clothes. Very unusual dream."

Claire smiled, unable to resist asking more. "What kind of clothes?"

Noah shrugged in thought. "Well, her shirt was skimpy and showed too much flesh, and she wore dungarees...but too tight and I've never seen a woman wear them before."

She nodded. "Yeah, jeans are very popular, and they're supposed to be tight."

"What?"

Claire licked her lips. "Remember, I'm from the future?"

Noah shook his head but then paused to stare into her eyes. "Did I dream of you?"

Not expecting the question, she didn't know what to say.

"Oh, my God!" Noah continued. "I didn't think anything of it at the time, since I fell asleep in front of the portrait, but the woman from my dream stood in front of it as well. Was she you, Claire?"

"I...I..." She still didn't know what to say. Why had he dreamt of her from the future? She shook her head and closed her eyes. "I don't know what all this means, Noah."

His hands moved to grip her arms. "I dreamt of you?"

Claire nodded without opening her eyes. "I don't know why, but yes, I think that was me...the real me."

"But how is that possible?" Noah gasped.

She slowly opened her eyes and shrugged with a small smile. "How is any of this possible?"

That question seemed to echo off the walls. They both nodded as Noah's hands dropped away from her. He shivered and looked at the fire. "Well, we best get things ready. When the sun sets, it will get awfully cold in here. We'll need more wood for the fire." He looked back at her. "Make yourself at home, and I'll be right back."

She nodded as she watched him stand and walk toward the door. He turned to look at her before he closed the door behind him. "If you really are from the future, then that wasn't a guess you made about Hank killing us, was it?"

Claire swallowed the lump in her throat as she shook her head.

Noah nodded slowly and cleared his throat. "I'll be outside if you need me."

Chapter 23

Claire stood in the small kitchen and looked around. She had never before felt so out of place. Noah had explained that the gas lines didn't reach out far enough to the cabin, so they had a wood-burning stove. Claire never thought she would see one of those relics, let alone actually be in the same room with one. She didn't know where to start. Luckily, Noah had gotten the fire started for her, but she didn't know how to cook on anything but electric. She had used a gas stove once or twice, but she felt way out of her depth.

The cabin's higher elevation made the air a bit chillier than in town. Claire stood closer to the heat coming from the old fashioned stove and rubbed her hands together. She stared at the kettle on the stovetop before turning to look at the sink. A hand pump sat beside it, which she assumed must be attached to an outside well. Her gaze moved to the small window, through which she could see Noah. He had stripped off his shirt to split wood with an ax, and she watched his muscles flex with each strike. In spite of the chill outside, she could see the perspiration on his chest and shoulders. He would need a shower when he finished his task.

Claire's eyes widened at the thought. She somehow doubted the cabin had indoor plumbing and went in search of the bathroom. All she found was a closet with a portable tub in it. A morbid thought occurred to her as she headed to the back door and pulled it open. She stepped out on the back porch and looked around until she found what she sought. As Claire stared at the outhouse, she groaned. "Oh, damn!" She muttered to herself, almost wishing they had stayed in Noah's office.

"What's wrong?" Noah asked as he rounded the back of the cabin carrying several logs of wood.

"I've never used an outhouse before."

Noah chuckled as he deposited the wood in the rack beside the door. "I'll make sure there are no spider webs or animals nesting before you need to use it." He gave her a sideways glance. "Unless you need to use it right now?"

She shook her head quickly, hoping the need would be long in coming. Her expression must have been horrified, since Noah straightened and gave her a concerned look.

"There are chamber pots in each of the bedrooms, but you would have to empty them after use. I suppose everyone has indoor plumbing in the future?"

Claire nodded and bit her lip. She sincerely hoped that Faith's menstrual cycle wasn't due anytime soon. She hadn't considered that and certainly didn't want to deal with it. She had the strongest desire to be back home. "Maybe staying here isn't such a good idea."

Noah sighed and wiped his hands on his pants. He looked around and took a deep breath. "I agree it's a bit rustic, but the weather is great. Bet you haven't smelled air that clear in a long time?"

Claire sniffed the air and then shrugged. She felt very near breaking down into sobs but hoped she could keep the urge at bay. They both had enough to worry about.

He walked closer and rubbed her arms. "I'll do most of the work around here, and if you need any help with something, let me know. You should probably stay here at least through the end of the week. I'll head back into town tomorrow and see if I can snoop around. I definitely have to let Mr. Baltimore know what's happened."

Her eyes widened. "You're going to leave me here? What if something happens to you? I would be stuck here."

Noah frowned. "Nothing is going to happen to me, Claire. Trust me."

"I do trust you. It's Hank that I'm worried about."

He shook his head. "I'll stay away from Hank, so don't worry."

"I can't help but worry," Claire sighed, realizing he was right. He couldn't neglect his job or responsibilities. Thoughts raced through her head. According to her dream of the events Faith had died first and then Noah had been killed. Claire had the idea that if Noah hadn't come along to witness Hank killing Faith, that he might have survived the ordeal. That made her think he would be safe on his own. Hank didn't really have any need to kill anyone at the moment. Faith wasn't his wife, so she should technically be safe as well. Though she knew that if the Pruitts got their hands on her, she would be forced into the marriage. "Just make sure you don't make any mention of knowing where I am…to anyone."

Noah smiled. "Of course not." He gave her arm a gentle squeeze. "Now, let me get back to work."

She nodded and tried to return his smile before heading back into the cabin. Not knowing what else to do, she walked into the main bedroom. She opened the closet and smiled upon seeing the old-fashioned hats and dresses. Claire reached for one of the hats and put it on her head. Turning toward the mirror, she chuckled upon seeing her reflection. Claire had never been a hat person though, so she took it off and put it back in the closet. Shutting the door, she walked over to the dresser. A little wooden chest sat on the left side, and Claire couldn't resist opening it to look inside. She gazed past the few pieces of costume jewelry to the decorated hairpins and smiled. Faith had long hair, and Claire hadn't thought to take any of the girl's hairpins with her when she had escaped her house.

She sifted through them until she found about half a dozen of the same style. They were all U-shaped and about three inches long, with a small blue butterfly at the top. Claire didn't want something that would scrape against her head, so she made sure they didn't have any rough edges or were too big. She gnawed on her lower lip as she poked the sharp ends, wondering at the possibility of it stabbing her scalp. Claire looked at one of the pins from every angle, before depositing them on top of the dresser. She would just have to take her chances. After twisting Faith's hair into a knot on top of her head, she began to stick the pins into the mound. She used all six, unsure of how many it would take to make it secure. Claire tilted her head from one side to the next, feeling pretty confident that the hair would stay put. Nodding, she closed the lid to the small chest and then left the room.

After all the wood had been cut, Noah walked into the cabin, his chest and brow damp with perspiration. Claire's eyes widened, and she absently licked her lips. She would never have thought that sweat could be sexy, but Noah changed her mind. He looked at her with a small smile and stared at the top of her head.

"You look like a librarian." He noted with a grin.

She blushed. "Well, it's the only way I knew to get this hair out of my face." Claire shrugged, wondering if she should take it down.

Noah chuckled. "I was just teasing. You look great. All those butterflies are a nice touch." He paused a moment longer to stare at her hair before turning toward the kitchen. "How many of them did you use?"

Claire bit her lip with a shrug. "Six," she called to his retreating back. "Is that too many?"

She followed him into the kitchen and watched him light the stove.

Noah chuckled. "I'm not sure what the style is, Claire, though I don't think my mother ever used that many." He pumped some water and put it on the stove to heat. "I don't think she'll mind, though." He added, giving her his most charming smile.

Once the water heated, Noah added it to the tub. He let her get cleaned up first and then he took his turn in the same water. She would have preferred a tub big enough for the both of them, but he waited for her to leave the room before he undressed.

That night they slept in separate bedrooms, since Claire didn't have the nerve to request they sleep in the same bed. She felt certain that Noah regretted their night together, especially since she had revealed to him who she really was. She didn't get much sleep that night, tossing and turning most of the time. Vague dreams plagued what little sleep she did get, and as dawn approached, she stared bleary eyed at the ceiling.

Claire wondered how early Noah would leave to head back to town. She hated the idea of being away from him, let alone having to spend the day by herself in the cabin. She couldn't exactly pass the time surfing the Internet or watching television. Claire clutched the covers above her, again almost wishing she were back home. She felt so out of place, and she couldn't imagine what she should do next.

Impulsively, she shoved back the covers and got out of bed. She winced as her feet hit the cold floor and looked around for socks or slippers. She found a pair at the foot of the bed and slipped them on.

Claire left her room and headed for Noah's. She tapped lightly on the door before pushing it open. Noah stood in front of the dresser buttoning his shirt. He turned to look at her with a slightly surprised expression.

"You're up early."

She licked her lips, almost dreading that he had already gotten out of bed. Claire swallowed the lump in her throat, wondering if she would have the nerve to slide in beside him had he still been asleep.

"I don't think I slept much last night."

Noah frowned. "Bad dreams?"

She shook her head. "I missed you…and now I won't even get to see you most of the day."

He sighed and turned away from the mirror. "Everything's gotten so complicated. I need my wits about me."

"And I make you witless?" Claire tried to joke but failed as her lower lip quivered.

Noah groaned softly as he stepped closer to her, "but in a good way," he nodded. He reached to cup her cheek in his hand. "What's wrong?"

She sighed at his touch and closed her eyes. "I don't know how much more time I have here, and I don't know how any of this is going to turn out. I just hate not being with you for any of it." Claire opened her eyes and looked up at his face.

He shook his head. "Well, I can't take you with me, and I can't stay here. What other solution is there?"

Claire bit her lower lip and took a deep breath. "You can spend some time with me before you leave." As she spoke, she moved a bit closer to him.

A slight smile touched his lips. "Is that really a good idea, Claire?"

She placed her hands on his chest, moving her fingers closer to the buttons on his shirt. "I love it when you call me by my name." Claire kissed the hollow of his neck and tentatively unfastened one of the buttons.

"Claire?" He asked but didn't stop her. Instead she leaned forward and kissed the bit of chest revealed to her. Claire could feel him quiver beneath her touch, and that pleased her.

"Do you want me to stop?" She asked as she let one of her hands slide down his body to rest between his legs. Noah sucked in his breath at her boldness, but he still didn't move. Claire smiled as she felt his arousal. "It doesn't feel like you do."

As an idea occurred to her, she got a bit nervous and wondered how shocking it would be to Noah. She slid her hand to the top of his slacks and began to unzip them. Noah's hand slipped to her shoulder and then back as she drew closer, and his fingers gripped the fabric of her pajama top.

"What are you doing?" He whispered.

Without meeting his gaze, she reached into his pants. "You gave me such pleasure the other night that I want to return the favor." Claire sighed as she wrapped her fingers around his erection and pulled it through the fly opening.

"I don't know how you could give me more pleasure than I already had."

She licked her lips with a smile as she finally met his gaze and dropped to her knees in front of him. "I'd like to try," she said as she stared up at him.

Noah looked confused at first. "What are you doing?"

"You'll see…and enjoy." She stroked him with her hand for a moment before breaking her gaze from his to lean forward and take him into her mouth.

Noah's whole body spasmed, and his hands went into her hair. "Claire, stop."

She grabbed hold of his thighs and suckled him. Noah groaned from above, and Claire hoped she did it right. Of course, she had never done such a thing before, but she didn't know of anyone else who deserved it more.

"Oh, Claire, oh my God!"

Noah began to tremble and let go of her hair. She felt something sharp against her scalp but didn't pay it any mind. He gripped the dresser beside him, and she tightened her hold on his legs. She wasn't sure how long it would take, but Noah didn't give her the opportunity to find out. He let out a growl and grabbed her arms to pull her to her feet. Without a word, he tore down her pajama bottoms and lifted her to the top of the dresser in the same movement. Once off her feet, he yanked her bottoms off the rest of the way and then slid in between her thighs. Before she even realized it would happen, he had buried himself within her. Claire gasped at the unexpected sensation of being impaled completely by him so quickly and then wrapped her arms around him. It only took a few thrusts before he gasped against her neck.

"Where on earth did you learn that?" He finally asked once he could speak.

Still being shook up by the passionate encounter, it took her a moment to respond. Claire was still a bit sore from their first time, and she realized that tears had formed in her eyes. She quickly wiped them away with a shrug. "I never really learned how. Was it alright?"

Noah pulled away with a short bark of laughter. "Are you kidding? I've never felt anything quite like it." He then noticed her tears. "Did I hurt you?" He groaned. "I acted like an uncivilized brute, didn't I? Damn…I never wanted to hurt you." He pulled her into a tight embrace, kissing her tears away.

She shook her head. "No, it was great. I just didn't expect it." Claire smiled and caressed his face. "I wanted to please you."

He kissed the palm of her hand and nodded. "Well, you did." He then leaned forward and kissed her. She sighed against his mouth, always loving the feel of him.

"I'll miss you today."

Noah gazed into her eyes for a moment. "I'll miss you too, but I'll be back before you know it." He gave her another quick kiss before helping her down from the dresser. Seeing her pajama bottoms on the bed behind him, he slipped his hand into the back pocket of his slacks as he reached for the bottoms. He then handed them to her with a sheepish grin. "I don't really know what to say. It's certainly not anything I'll ever forget."

Claire grinned. "Neither will I."

Chapter 24

After Noah left, Claire stared into the mirror and shook her head as she realized she hadn't taken her hair down the previous night. She removed the hairpins from her messy hair and stared at them, realizing how lucky she'd been that one or all of them hadn't stabbed her while she slept. After she had removed five pins, she frowned when she didn't come across the sixth one. Claire looked at the floor of both rooms before giving up, figuring it would turn up eventually. She brushed her hair and then put the hair back up, reinserting the hairpins. After that, she cleaned herself up as best she could with a bucket of water, not wanting to heat up enough to fill the portable tub. Once dressed, she stood on the back porch and tossed the used water into the back yard. Not knowing how else to spend her day, she looked around and wondered if she should tour the area. Noah had mentioned a lake, which certainly must be nearby. Claire stared at the trees and wondered if they hid her view of it.

She stared into the cabin behind her and gnawed on her lower lip. She knew of nothing to do in there. Sighing, Claire figured she might as well be adventurous. She didn't know how much longer she had in 1935 before she would be sent home and wouldn't have the luxury of being able to walk freely through the wilderness. A smile touched her lips at her own reference. Noah had called the place rustic, but it felt like the backwoods of some uncharted forest.

Trees stretched out in all directions, so she didn't really know which direction to try. Claire wondered if she should leave breadcrumbs to help find her way back. A chuckle escaped at the thought, which helped lighten her mood.

Deciding to walk in the opposite direction of the outhouse, she set off. After only a few minutes, she ran across a dirt trail that cut through the trees. Claire turned to look over her shoulder, relieved to still see the cabin. Taking a left on the trail, her mind wandered. Would Noah truly avoid Hank, or would he confront him? Would he be safe or might Hank harm him?

She felt a burst of anger flow through her at the thought of Hank harming Noah. The dream of Noah's and Faith's deaths went through her mind. Hank killed Faith and then Noah had stumbled across the scene. He had obviously been taken by surprise and didn't expect the attack, but now Noah knew that Hank could be a danger to them both. Maybe that knowledge would save him. Since she didn't know what she would do if anything happened to him, she certainly hoped so.

When the lake appeared before her, Claire gasped. She didn't know what she had expected, but the immense body of water took her breath away. The sunlight shimmered across the smooth surface. A small twenty-foot dock had been built from the edge of the lake, and Claire walked to the end of it. She took off her shoes and sat with her feet in the cool water. She looked around and couldn't see anyone else, not even a lone fisherman, though the other docks in the distance housed several boats. Claire assumed that autumn must be off-season for the lake's inhabitants.

She placed her arms behind her and leaned back against them to stare up at the blue sky. The birds chirped in the trees and a breeze blew through her hair. Claire could understand why Noah's parents enjoyed the cabin so much with the lake being a hidden paradise. If she enjoyed fishing, she would be in heaven. Claire dropped her chin to stare across the lake. She knew the water would feel wonderful to swim in. She stared down at her feet and watched a little fish suck on one of her toes. Claire's eyes widened as she fought the impulse to kick it away. Instead she just watched it and then giggled as it swam between her toes. A shiver went up her spine, and she finally moved her feet to scare it away.

Hunger drove her away from the lake hours later. As she gave it one last glance over her shoulder, Claire realized she would spend most of her free time there. She wondered if Noah's mother might have left a bathing suit at the cabin.

Once she got back, she fixed something to eat and then went in search of a bathing suit. Disappointment flooded her when she couldn't find one. Claire wondered if she had the nerve to swim in her underwear. She would certainly have no qualms doing that in the 21st century, but who knew how it would be looked at in the early 20th century. Her face brightened at the thought of swimming at night.

Claire didn't know what else to do with her day. Deciding that she may as well take care of some of the dust, she cleaned up the cabin as best she could. Feeling a bit chilly, she put more logs in the fireplace and rubbed her hands together to get warm. After running out of things to do, she lay down on the couch with an afghan and closed her eyes. She didn't feel tired, but almost as soon as her eyes closed, she fell asleep.

The dream started out normal enough. She was back in her own body, but when she looked into the mirror, she saw Faith's reflection. The mirror slowly morphed into the portrait, and she gripped the edges of it and shook it.

"Why did you do this to me? I want Noah! I need him!" She suddenly let go of the portrait as if it burnt her, crossing her arms over her chest. The tears streamed down her face as she looked upward and screamed, "Noah! Come back to me, Noah!"

Claire sat up with a strangled cry, looking around the room with panicked eyes. Her gaze stopped on the portrait, before she threw aside the afghan and stumbled across the room. She stopped in front of the wrapped bundle and began to tear off the paper. Once she could see Faith's face, she gripped the edges of the frame.

"What are you trying to tell me, Faith?" Reliving her dream, Claire jumped back and let go of the portrait as if it burnt her. She rubbed her hands together, afraid to touch it again. "What do you have planned for us?" The tears misting her eyes surprised her as she crossed her arms over her chest. Not wanting to take the chance of touching the portrait, Claire took a few steps back. She dropped to her knees in front of it and glared at Faith.

She had no way of knowing when Noah would be back, but her dream prompted fear within her. She needed to see him in the worst way. Not having any way of reaching him was insufferable. Claire felt totally helpless, and the tears began to roll down her cheeks. She had known that falling in love with him would be a bad idea, but she had been unable to control herself. Telling him that she loved him before she even met him had been the truth, of course, so she realized there had been no way to stop the inevitable. She now also feared heartbreak, which she knew was just as inevitable.

Claire didn't know how long she sat staring at the portrait. Being so lost in thought, she didn't realize the sound she heard was of a door being opened and closed. By the time the sound did register in her clouded brain, he stood behind her. Claire smiled her relief as she spun around at the waist, getting ready to stand and then throw herself into Noah's arms. She froze with a gasp to see Hank standing there. Still being seated became a disadvantage as he moved closer to her. Claire tried to bolt away, but he reached down and grabbed one of her ankles. Her terror prevented her from screaming.

Hank grabbed her back toward him as he knelt beside the couch. "Is this any way to greet your fiancé?"

Claire couldn't believe he had found her and shook her head. Could she still be dreaming? Her lungs felt as if they would collapse, and she suddenly realized she hadn't breathed since she saw him. She sucked in air and tried to scream, when he pounced on her and covered her mouth with one of his hands. The other hand reached into his pocket and pulled out a cloth, which Hank held in front of her eyes.

"And here I thought I would be marrying a virgin. Guess it doesn't really matter though, does it?"

Claire's eyes widened as she focused on the torn pair of panties she had thrown in the trash at Noah's office. She tried to speak through his hand, but he shook his head.

"You're not going to scream, are you?" When she shook her head, he moved his hand to her neck.

Claire swallowed the lump in her throat. "Is Noah OK?"

He gave her an evil grin. "Now that depends entirely on you." His gaze moved beyond her. "I see you brought our wedding present with you. Isn't that fitting?" He looked away from the portrait and back into her terror stricken eyes. "You just delayed it, my dear. Our wedding is still going to happen."

She began to shake her head again, but he grabbed her shirt by the collar and pulled her face within an inch of his. "If you don't want anything to happen to your lover, you will go along with anything I ask of you."

Not having a rebuttal to that, she laid silently as he tied her wrists together behind her back. He kept hold of the other end of the rope and jerked her to her feet. Hank grabbed the portrait and put it under his other arm. He then tugged on the rope and led her toward the convertible parked out front of the cabin. Claire had never seen the sports car before but shook her head as Hank opened the driver's side door. She barely registered the fact that the door opened the wrong way as he leaned into the car and pulled the front seat forward, revealing a storage compartment behind it.

Claire put up a mild struggle as he pushed her toward the compartment, but he easily picked her up and deposited her inside. He then took the rope and tied the other end around her ankles.

"Hank, why do you have to marry me? Can't you just let us be? It isn't too late."

He looked at her for a moment before leaning forward to shove the torn underwear into her mouth. Claire tried to shake her head, but he tightened his hold on her face and shoved the cloth in deeper. She thought she would gag.

"It *is* too late…for you anyway. You will be my wife, Faith, one way or another!" He then gave her a twisted smile, and she looked into his soulless eyes with a shudder. She had almost forgotten that he was a monster!

The seat moved back into place and engulfed her in darkness.

Chapter 25

With enough effort Claire succeeded in pushing the panties from her mouth with her tongue. She spat it out and then coughed a few times. Rolling onto her back, she tried to look around the cramped area. With her knees bent at an uncomfortable angle, she winced as her bound wrists scraped against something beneath her.

As she thought about her situation, she bitterly fought tears. Claire refused to let Hank see her cry, no matter how bad it got. He had really gone over the edge, and she wondered how he found her. How had he found her panties? Claire gasped as she realized he must know about Noah's office. Did that mean that he had found Noah there as well? She swallowed the painful lump in her throat as she prayed that he still lived.

Time had no meaning as the car continued to its destination. The muffled sound of the radio played some old tune, and Claire vaguely wondered if the compartment had enough air. Could his plan be to let her suffocate? She sighed and wondered where Hank was taking her. She hated the unknown and kicked the other side of the car in her frustration. Her eyes lit up as she felt it move slightly. She then began kicking at it in earnest with the heels of her shoes. Claire bit her lip as she hoped Hank couldn't hear or feel her efforts.

He could pull over the car and finish her off. She shook her head. Hank wouldn't kill her until after he married her, so she should be safe. At least that is what she told herself as she continued kicking.

It finally gave way, and Claire winced at the sound of the little door swinging open and hitting the outside of the car. As the fresh air hit her face, she sucked in a deep breath but then held it. She waited for the skid of tires as Hank pulled the car over, but the sound never came. Realizing that between the sounds of the engine and radio, he probably couldn't hear anything else. Claire let out her breath and frowned. What could she do? More light shone inside, but she couldn't exactly escape through that small hole, especially from a speeding car. As she stared out the opening, she could see that Hank drove very fast. Grunting in frustration, she moved closer to the opening and tried to fit her feet through the hole. Luckily, Faith had small feet, and she could get both of them through. Once they dangled outside, she wiggled her feet.

"Damn!" She muttered. Unless someone happened to be driving behind them, no one would even notice. If Hank drove too fast in the Speedster, she doubted a cop could keep up. Realizing she would have to face Hank's wrath when he let her out, Claire rolled her eyes. "Who gives a shit?" She muttered again, realizing he couldn't do worse to her than he already had planned.

Her eyes misted as her thoughts turned to Noah. She thought of their time together that morning. Claire's chest tightened at the thought of something happening to him. She shouldn't have let him leave the cabin.

Time dragged by slowly as she mentally beat herself up for involving him at all. The car finally stopped, and Claire sucked in her breath.

"What the hell?" Hank's voice yelled out from beyond her feet.

In the next moment the seat moved aside, and he glared angrily at her. "Do you know how much that will cost to get fixed?" He asked as he looked at the broken lock on the storage compartment door.

Claire shook her head silently, fighting the urge to tell him that she didn't care. Hank shook his head in disgust and reached for her. Noticing the panties beside her, he frowned. "Are you going to scream?"

She shook her head again. He contemplated her for a moment before grabbing the panties and shoving them into his pocket. He then untied the rope around her ankles and pulled her from the car. Claire groaned at his roughness and looked around. When she realized they were at Hank's house, she looked at him. "What's next, Hank?"

"We have a wedding to get ready for. I have your dress laid out for you in our room."

Claire coughed. "Our room?"

He nodded with a devilish grin. "Well, it will be soon enough."

"You can't really expect to marry me, do you?"

Hank tugged on the rope, and she winced. The muscles in her arms and shoulders screamed, and she felt like screaming right along with them. Instead she followed him into the house.

He shrugged. "I guess that all depends on you."

Claire's eyes widened. "Where's Noah?"

"He's around."

"Here?"

He shrugged again, and Claire narrowed her eyes. "You know I won't do anything you ask of me, unless I know he's alright."

Hank tugged sharply on the rope, causing her to yelp in surprise and pain. "I'm counting on it," he responded through clenched teeth. The sweet smell should have warned her, but the cloth over her face surprised her. She involuntarily sucked in her breath to scream, but that proved to be a mistake. Everything went black.

When she came to, Claire felt something very soft beneath her. She rolled over with a groan and looked around the spacious and luxurious room. When she focused on the white dress beside her on the bed, she gasped and rolled away from it. Gooseflesh rose on her arms, and she rubbed them as her hair fell across her face. Claire moved it out of the way and then felt for the back of her head. The hairpins had been removed. She shook her head in disgust, knowing that Hank had been the thief. She figured he couldn't take the chance of her using them as weapons. Gritting her teeth, she looked across the room and noticed a large tub in front of the fireplace. Claire walked over to it and stuck a finger into the water. The temperature felt lukewarm at best but at least not cold. Someone had recently prepared the bath for her, and she wondered if Hank had actually been the one to do it. Somehow she couldn't imagine him in the kitchen heating water, which brought up the idea that a maid might help her. She bit her lip as she turned around and glanced at the windows. Claire doubted she occupied a room on the first floor and wondered if she would break anything by jumping from the second or third floor.

She approached the window and pushed aside the curtain. Where it had been late in the day, it now looked to be morning. Whatever Hank had drugged her with had knocked her out all night. At least she hoped it had only been one night, which would currently make it Friday. As she stared down at the ground far below, she bit her lip. She was on the third floor. Her gaze moved away from outside to her hand holding the curtain. The ropes that had bound her the previous day had been removed, but she could still see the chafed marks on her wrist. She absently rubbed them and wondered what to do.

When the door opened, Claire realized she had run out of time. She spun around and faced Hank as he walked in carrying her portrait. He barely spared her a glance before placing it on the mantel above the fireplace. She watched him silently for a moment, before approaching the tub. "Is this supposed to be for me?"

Hank stared up at the painting for a moment before looking at her over his shoulder. When he saw her gesture toward the tub, he nodded. "I want to make sure you wash well, too, dear. I want all traces of that man off of you."

She cringed. "Why do you want me so clean? Do you plan on eating me?" As soon as that last question left her mouth, she gasped and her stomach clenched. Though she had meant the statement one way, it could be taken another way, and she certainly didn't want him having sexual thoughts about her. Claire frowned, not sure if anyone even practiced that kind of foreplay in the 30's. Not wanting to leave that hanging in the air, she quickly added, "I would hope you would cook me well first."

Hank chuckled in surprise. "No, I'm not a cannibal, Faith! Such ideas and such a silly girl." He walked closer to her and tugged on a lock of her hair. "I want you clean for our wedding night."

Claire gasped. "You can't be serious."

He smiled. "Of course, I am. This will be a real marriage, and don't act naïve now. After all, you know what goes on between a man and a woman."

She shook her head but couldn't say anything.

"I have to say I was a bit surprised at my discovery in the trash. I thought for sure that you and Janet…unless you actually prefer both men and women? Are you that confused, Faith, that you can't pick?"

"But you're only marrying me so that you can kill me," she finally sputtered.

Hank grasped her arms tightly. "Where on earth did you get that idea?"

"How did you find my panties?" She countered.

He frowned at the subject change before turning away with a shrug and a wave of his hand. "I've suspected that Noah had a hidden agenda for awhile now. I couldn't prove it, and I wasn't actually going to do anything about it…that is until you ran off." Hank sat on the edge of the tub and glowered at her. Claire stared back, wishing she had the courage to scratch his eyes out.

He sighed. "I saw him leave his office one day. I waited and eventually his secretary left. I followed her to a nearby pub. She is quite pretty and enjoyed being flirted with. Eventually with a few drinks, she opened up to me about her employer. When you ran off, I went to his office to see if you were there. If I hadn't had to use the toilet, I might not have found your unmentionables in the trash." He reached into his pocket and pulled out her panties. He looked at them and ran his finger over the embroidered letters before meeting her gaze. "It was quite stupid of you to leave them there, especially with your monogram on them." He held them up so she could see, and Claire's eyes widened. How had she never noticed the small FP on the upper left side of the panties? Hank smiled to see her surprise as his gaze dropped back to the cloth in his hand. "Nancy was also shocked when I confronted her with them. She didn't want to tell me where you were, though I did manage to scare the information out of her."

Claire gasped. "You didn't hurt her, did you?"

He shook his head. "Of course not. Do you think I'm crazy?"

She nodded against her will but then bit her lower lip. Hank grinned at her. "That's right, you think I'm just marrying you so I can kill you. Let's just say that I doubt she stuck around. Noah will probably have to find himself a new secretary…if he still needs one after..."

Claire frowned as chills went up her spine. "After what?"

"After all this is said and done." He straightened and shoved himself away from the tub. "Now you need to bathe."

"Where is Noah?" She repeated.

"I'll take you to him after you've cleaned up." With that said, he left the room without a backward glance. Once the door closed behind him, she stared at the portrait on the mantel. Faith's lost look took on new meaning as a lost Claire began to take off her clothes.

After her bath, she put on a robe she found. Claire refused to put on the wedding dress until she had to. When Hank came to collect her, the disapproval shown across his face at her attire. "Why aren't you dressed?"

Claire looked at the white dress on the bed and shrugged. "Are you sure white is the proper color?"

Not expecting such a response, he chuckled. "Yeah, you probably should wear red, but white is custom. No one else needs to know what you've been up to. Now are you going to get dressed, or do I need to help you?" He added threateningly.

She cringed and crossed her arms over her chest. "You told me that you'd take me to Noah. I need to make sure he's OK."

Hank nodded. "Yes, I did say that, didn't I? Alright, let's go." He stepped aside and gestured toward the door. "Now don't try to run away. All the doors are locked, and I'm a fast runner."

Claire looked at him and licked her dry lips. "I'm not going anywhere until I know that Noah is safe."

"Isn't that sweet?" He again gestured toward the door. She walked through first and then let out a scream as a blindfold came over her eyes. Claire held up her hands to push it away, but then Hank tightened his hold on her and hissed in her ear. "Silence!" He growled. "I don't want you to know where he is. Do you want to see your lover or not?"

The blindfold terrified her, but she nodded and let him tie it around her head. He then took her by the arm and led her through the house. They went down a flight of stairs and then another flight of stairs. Claire lost track of the times they turned and began to think he deliberately tried to mess with her sense of direction. They went up a flight of stairs and then stopped, and she heard a key in a lock and a door pushed open. Hank's hand on her back moved her through the doorway.

It took a moment before she could focus once the blindfold had been removed, and her gaze riveted to a horrible sight in the middle of the room. Noah looked unharmed, with his arms tied behind his back and a noose around his neck. When Claire's gaze dropped down his body to his feet, she sucked in her breath. He stood on top of a large block of ice, which had already begun to melt. Water pooled around and sunk into the rug beneath it. A chair lay on its side a few feet from the block of ice. She took the scene in and shook her head, ready to spring across the room, but Hank's strong hand on her arm stopped her.

"Noah?" Her strangled cry sounded pitiful even to her own ears.

"I'm alright! Has he hurt you?" Noah asked her as his gaze went from her face down to her feet and then back up.

Claire shook her head, fighting the tears misting her eyes. "He found your office." She said miserably, not stating it as a question, but Noah nodded.

"The bastard jumped me from behind. The next thing I knew I was here."

Claire bit her lip and stared again at the ice. Once it melted to a certain level, Noah would hang, and slowly at that. Hank wouldn't even need to be in the same state when it happened, and Claire had no idea how long it would take to melt the ice.

She shivered as Hank moved closer to whisper in her ear. "I'll light the fire before we leave today, and that ice will melt in no time.

Claire gave the fireplace a quick glance before she spun around to face him. "How can you do this? What is wrong with you?" She spat at him in anger and frustration. "What did we ever do to you?"

Hank looked sympathetic for a moment before he shook his head. "You are just a means to an end...but him?" He pointed at Noah. "He betrayed me. He was supposed to be my friend, and he tried to steal you away from me."

"But why did you choose me? What's so special about me?" She asked him, stealing another look at Noah over her shoulder. Claire hated wasting time, but she had no idea how to save him.

"You're wasting time, Faith." Hank told her, following her gaze to Noah as if reading her mind. "How much time do you think he has? I won't cut him down until after we're married. So, if by some chance, the wedding doesn't take place, guess what happens?"

Claire gasped and sharply returned her gaze to him. "That's extortion...or blackmail. Hell, I don't know what it's called, but it's not fair!" She felt like stomping her foot. She sucked air into her lungs in short gasps and feared she might hyperventilate.

"Who said life is fair?" Hank asked softly.

Chapter 26

Claire sat on the bed in her room, dressed in the white dress. She stared down at the fabric and lightly caressed it. Under different circumstances she might even have liked the pretty dress, but she couldn't see past the ugliness of the situation. She was being forced to marry a monster to save the man she loved. It sounded like a bad soap opera, and she wanted to curl into a ball in a corner and cry.

Instead she sat on the bed and waited for Hank to fetch her. He hadn't even let her tell Noah goodbye before putting the blindfold back on and then dragging her away from the room. Claire licked her dry lips at the cruel memory. As far as she knew it had been the last time she would set eyes on Noah. Her gaze rose to meet Faith's in the portrait. "What now?" She asked aloud. "Any tips? I'm about to get you married to the man that will kill you." Claire so badly wanted to cry but she refused to give into the weakness. If she started now, she wouldn't be able to stop.

How had things gotten so bad? She had been sent back to stop the marriage, but she failed. It was even happening a day ahead of schedule. Claire didn't look up when the door opened. Expecting Hank, she started upon seeing a young woman walk in. The girl wore a maid's uniform, and Claire stared at her. She couldn't understand why Hank would allow someone to come into the room with her.

It took a moment of indecision before Claire sprang from the bed and ran over to the maid, who seemed quite shocked at the quick approach.

"I'm sorry, but you need to help me. Noah, the other man who has been staying here, is in trouble. Do you know where he is?"

The maid frowned at her but didn't answer. "What's wrong with you?" Claire asked her.

"She doesn't speak English."

Claire almost screamed in surprise and turned toward the door. Hank stood in the doorway and smirked at her. "You must think I'm dumb, too." He chuckled before turning to the maid to speak to her. Claire didn't recognize the language, but she shook her head in defeat.

When Hank finished talking to the maid, the young woman left the room. Claire watched her go before turning a heated gaze on Hank, who smiled at her. "Well, you ready for your big day? Everyone is assembled and awaiting you. I must say that it took quite a bit of persuasion to keep your mother downstairs."

Claire sucked in her breath. "The Pruitts are here?"

Hank nodded, seemingly oblivious to her calling them by their last name. "Of course they are. They're the witnesses, after all." He held out his arm. "Shall we? We're cutting it close."

She glared at him and headed for the door. Hank grabbed her wrist and pulled her back. "You will act like you're happy about this marriage. I want them all to believe it." He hissed at her, "or Noah will suffer for it."

Claire sucked in her breath and glared at him. "He will anyway, won't he?"

"I'll hold up my end of the bargain, Faith. Now put on a happy face."

She knew he lied but also knew she didn't have a choice. Claire swallowed the lump in her throat and slid her arm through his, so that he could lead her downstairs.

The next few minutes passed in a blur. Claire would never have considered herself an actress, but she had to tolerate the hugs and kisses from Margie and Hector. After what they had put her through, she wanted to pull away from every show of affection. She knew that Hank watched her like a hawk, so she went through the motions. As it took every bit of concentration not to flee or yell out, she missed most of the conversation. The priest awaited her as well and introduced himself, and she shook his hand but couldn't look him in the eye.

They went through their vows, and Claire felt bile rise in her throat. The man she loved and wanted to marry stood on a melting block of ice somewhere above her, and she couldn't do anything to help him. If she yelled out that he needed help, who would believe her? She doubted the Pruitts would, since they would probably treat her like she was crazy. If by some chance someone actually listened to her, by the time they actually searched the house and found Noah, he would be dead. By then the ice would have melted and evaporated, and it would look like Noah had killed himself. As she again visualized him standing on that block of ice, a nagging doubt tried to surface in her mind. Something had been wrong with the suicide scenario, but she couldn't piece that part of the puzzle together.

Claire truly felt wedged between a rock and a hard place. She knew that Hank only wanted to marry her so that he could kill her, but she could only hope that somehow she could save Noah. When it came time to sign the marriage license, she picked up the pen and almost didn't hear Margie's voice.

"Honey, what are you doing? You're left handed."

Claire looked at her with a frown before slowly moving the pen from her right to her left hand. She hadn't known that Faith was left-handed. As she awkwardly held the pen, she contemplated what to sign on the license. Knowing that it wouldn't be legible no matter what she signed, she scrawled Faith Todds.

When she straightened and met Hank's gaze, he stared at her suspiciously before looking down at her signature. Claire held her breath, wondering if he had ever seen Faith sign her name. He frowned but didn't say anything as he signed his name beneath hers.

She let out her breath as she watched the Pruitts sign as witnesses. They must surely have seen Faith's signature, but neither commented on her scrawl. Claire felt light headed as they hugged her again, congratulating her on her marriage.

"He's a fine catch, Faith. I'm glad you finally came around." Margie whispered in her ear. Claire had to bite her tongue not to respond, but then Hector hugged her.

"Make me proud, girl." His gruff voice told her. Claire felt that bile rise again and forced a nod.

"I'm sure I will," she muttered, not knowing how much more she could take. She floated through the next hour as everyone toasted the marriage. Margie brought a cake, and they all had a slice. Claire had to bite her lip to keep from shouting at them all, but she managed to hold herself together.

After what seemed an eternity, Hank walked everyone to the door for the farewells. "Well, I would like to spend some time alone with my wife. Thank you all for coming."

Claire closed her eyes as she listened to their small talk. She could think of nothing but Noah slowly choking to death, and they laughed and carried on like idiots. She stared up at the ceiling and clenched her teeth. When she heard the door close, her gaze returned to Hank.

"So now you'll let Noah go?"

He loosened his tie and then his cufflinks as he returned her stare. "Now why would I do that?"

"Because you promised," she gasped.

"I promised?" He asked with a smile. "I don't remember promising. I said I'd cut him down after we were married. I didn't specify when." He approached her slowly. Claire felt like a deer caught in headlights, but she pulled herself together and made a run for the stairs. Hank grabbed her and pulled her against his chest, tightening his hold on her. "I didn't go to all that trouble to let him go, my dear wife. We'll be on our honeymoon when he hangs. Everyone will think he hung himself. Poor Noah. I'll be appropriately mournful…so distraught."

It was then that she remembered Noah's hands tied behind his back. It couldn't very well look like a suicide, if the police found him bound and hung. Claire inwardly groaned, wondering if that would have made a difference had she remembered during the wedding. "It won't look like an accident!" She blurted without thought and then wished she could take the words back.

Hank stared at her for a moment before chuckling. "Of course, it will! After I stoke the fireplace, I will simply drug him again and then remove the ropes from his wrists. By the time the drug wears off…well, let's just say he won't be waking up, and I won't be anywhere nearby."

Her eyes widened. She wanted to spit in his face, but her mouth had gone dry. "You're a damn monster."

He suddenly kissed her. It shocked Claire so much that she couldn't react at first. She was about to bite him when he pulled back and licked his lips.

"I just realized I didn't get to kiss you after the ceremony. That makes it official."

"Please, Hank, don't do this."

He looked almost sad as he stared down into her misty eyes. "You know I can't let him go. I can't risk him going to the authorities. I can't leave any witnesses. He knows too much... so do you."

With that he clamped onto her wrist and drug her upstairs. She fought him for a few steps but then gave up. He was too strong, and she needed to think. She needed to sort her thoughts and come up with a solution.

By the time they reached their bedroom, she said the only thing she could think of. "I'm from the future!" She yelled out.

Hank scoffed at her and began to remove his shirt.

"I am! I know how you die. It's awful."

He smiled at her. "Oh really? How do I die?"

Claire swallowed the lump in her throat and said the first thing that came to her mind. "You get hit by a car."

"Wow, that's amazing." He tossed his shirt over a nearby chair before pausing to look her over.

She didn't like his lecherous stare and blurted more lies. "You don't die right away either. The car crushes your hips and legs. There's a lot of internal bleeding and damage. You'll be in constant pain until you die a few days later." Tears nearly sprang to her eyes as she remembered the pain she had been in after Hank's car had run her down. How she wished that had truly been his fate as well.

Hank frowned at her before shaking his head. “These stall tactics will not work, Faith. You have the choice of either undressing yourself or having me do it for you. This marriage will be consummated. You're my wife and will do as I say.”

She shook her head. “You're crazy. You think I will submit to you while Noah could be strangling?”

Hank shrugged. “That ice won't melt for hours. Like I said, we'll be long gone before that happens. Now get over here. It won't take long and then we'll be on our way. I want to get it over with before we leave. We'll be in the car for hours, and I'll be too tired to perform when we get there.”

“Where?”

“You know very well where we are going! It's been planned for over a month.”

Claire gasped. He planned to take her to the lake resort where he had originally killed Faith. She shook her head. “I won't go there.”

Hank sighed, clearly running out of patience. He crossed the room in a few strides and spun her around. Claire let out a scream as he ripped her dress open down her back. She tried to run, but he grabbed a handful of her hair and pulled her with him to the bed. He then threw her across the quilt and landed on top of her.

“God no, you can't do this!” She sobbed.

Hank ignored her as he began tearing the dress from her body. “Stop fighting me, Faith. It will be much easier on us both. It doesn't have to be rough, you know?"

Realizing she was about to cry, she bit down on her lip to ward off the tears. Hank moved between her legs and unfastened his pants. Claire closed her eyes and tried to remain calm. The next thing she knew, the weight of his body fell onto hers and was then quickly removed.

Claire opened her eyes to see two men roll off the bed. She sat up with a gasp, not even caring that she was almost naked. Hank and Noah rolled on the floor in a death grip. Noah still had rope tied around his wrists as he pummeled Hank's face, who quickly got over his surprise and began to fight back. Claire pulled the torn edges of her dress together and got off the bed to get a better look at them, unsure of what to do. She felt she should run and get help, but she didn't want to leave Noah alone with Hank. She sucked in her breath and continued to watch them.

"How on earth did you free yourself, Noah? I guess I underestimated you." Hank said with a groan as he avoided getting punched in the face.

Noah got hit in the chin, but he blocked the next punch and then managed to kick Hank away. "I think we both are a bit guilty of that."

Hank sneered as he lunged toward him to strike him in the face. Not knowing how much more of this she could bare, Claire ran over and jumped onto Hank's back, grasping handfuls of his hair. He yelled out in pain and rammed back against the nearest wall. Claire wrapped one arm around his neck and continued to pull his hair with the other, but he bent over and flipped her over him to land on the floor.

"Damn you, woman!" Hank growled and reached into his boot. She felt the breath knocked out of her as she watched him pull out a small pistol. Claire gasped and bolted to her feet, thinking only to stop Hank, who pointed the gun at her and pulled the trigger. Noah acted instinctively and jumped between Hank and Claire. He struck out at Hank as the bullet hit him and threw him backwards into Claire. As Hank fell from the solidly placed punch, Claire and Noah sunk to the floor in each other's arms.

"Noah?" She screamed as she clung to him. She stared at his chest and watched the red bloom across his shirt. "No, this can't be happening!"

Noah shook his head. "Don't worry about me. Only a flesh wound."

Claire tried to laugh but cried instead. "I don't think so, hon." She placed her hand over the bullet wound and pressed down. Noah grimaced in pain but shook his head.

"I'm sorry I failed, Claire. Don't let Hank get away with this." His hand reached up to squeeze hers, and she squeezed it back.

"I won't. I love you, Noah." Claire wanted to make sure he heard her, so she said it again. "I love you so much. It can't end like this." She sputtered through her tears.

He smiled at her. "It won't end. I'll follow you through time, if I have to. I won't ever leave you, Claire...I promise." Blood filled his mouth and trickled out the side. Claire shook her head as his hand fell away from her.

"Noah, please, hold on." She knew there wasn't anything that could be done. If they were in her future, he might have a chance. Claire hugged him tighter, not realizing at first that he had left something in the hand he had squeezed. Hank's voice surprised her.

"Well, that was unexpected."

She raised her head to glare at him as her fingers massaged the object in her hand. Her hatred shown clearly in her gaze, and his eyes widened.

"Why did he call you Claire?" He asked as he slowly approached her, still aiming the pistol at her.

She never looked away from his face. "That's my name," she responded in a mechanical voice. "Remember, I'm from the future."

Hank frowned, and the gun faltered in his grasp. He knelt beside them and leaned forward to feel for Noah's pulse. In that instant Claire reacted, slamming her hand into Hank's face. The hairpin that she held went into Hank's eye, and he fell back with a yell. His body began to twitch and then it went still.

She could only stare at him at first. Had she actually killed him? Not really caring, she turned her attention back to Noah, who smiled at her. "I thought that would come in handy again," he rasped, more blood trickling out of his mouth. She could see his eyes growing dim.

The tears fell down her face unchecked as she bent down to kiss him. As she descended toward him, a breeze blew through the room and knocked Faith's portrait off the mantel. It landed in front of them, and Claire raised a hand in defense. As soon as her fingers touched the painting, she felt herself being pulled into it. Claire shook her head and tightened her other arm around Noah.

"No!" She opened her mouth to scream and then all went black.

Chapter 27

Claire opened her eyes and stared at the ceiling. She blinked a few times and then licked her unusually dry lips.

"She's awake!"

The voice came from her right, and Claire turned in that direction to see her mother.

"Mom!" She cried and sat up, reaching for the older woman. They embraced, and Claire hung on tight. "Oh, my God, it's good to see you again."

The force of her sobs surprised everyone in the room. Claire's father, and her best friend, Stefanie, stood at the foot of the bed. Claire looked at them and couldn't stop crying. Everyone took turns hugging her before she finally took note of her surroundings, suddenly realizing that she lay in a hospital room. "Was it all a dream?"

She told herself that it couldn't be and fiercely shook her head. The memory of Noah dying in her arms was just too vivid. The thought of him brought fresh tears to her eyes.

"Honey, what's wrong? Was what a dream?" Her mother asked her, hugging her tighter.

Claire shook her head, looking from one face to the next. Her sister and brother weren't there, and she watched her father pull out his cell phone to call them. Stefanie stood wringing her hands, as if feeling out of place among the family. Claire reached out and clasped hands with her friend. "Why am I here?" Claire finally asked, feeling that she may as well start with being in a hospital. What had happened while she had been gone? Had any time elapsed?

"You passed out a week ago and wouldn't wake up…at least until now. None of the doctors could explain it." Her mother provided.

"I passed out a week ago?" She repeated slowly, trying to absorb that information. Claire had been sent back to 1935 a week ago, so her body had been unconscious the entire time she had been away? That meant that she and Faith hadn't changed places or that the younger girl had been trapped in a comatose body the entire time. Claire cringed at the idea, hoping that hadn't happened. "I've been here for a week?"

Another option occurred to her. She really had gone into a coma and had dreamt the whole time traveling thing. Claire sucked in her breath. That couldn't be possible, could it? She shook her head and swallowed the lump in her throat. How could she have had such a vivid dream? Falling in love with Noah, making love and then watching him die had to be real, didn't it? All the tears she had held in continued to stream down her face. "It had to be real," Claire moaned and looked at her mother. "Didn't I move out and rent that old house? Didn't I find a portrait?"

Her mother frowned. "What old house? You've lived with Stefanie since you went away to college. Don't you remember, honey?"

"Oh, my God!" Claire said with a gasp and stared at Stefanie, realizing that she did remember it. That and a whole lot of other memories flooded her mind. She saw things she had never known before, things she didn't remember doing, but they were in her head. "What's going on?" She leaned forward and pushed her palms into her temples, beginning to moan. She barely heard her father yell for help. This time Claire welcomed the blissful darkness that came for her.

When she opened her eyes again, she looked around the empty room. The tears had dried on her face as she sat up and looked at her covered legs. For the first time since waking in the hospital, Claire realized she did not feel pain in her hips and legs. She had almost gotten used to not feeling pain in Faith's body, but now she knew why she didn't feel the usual pain in her own body. Claire tried to smile as she pulled from her old memories, especially one from ten years earlier. She had looked both ways before crossing the street, but there hadn't been a car driven by an old man to run her down. Hank hadn't been alive to be behind the wheel of that BMW, because Claire had killed him.

Tears threatened to fill her eyes again, but she fought them off. She had apparently succeeded in her mission of saving Faith by killing that monster, but she had been unable to save Noah. He had died by jumping in the way of a bullet meant for her. Knowing she wouldn't be able to hold off the tears by thinking of him, she forced herself to think of Faith. Claire wondered whatever happened to her. Her family had owned the house she rented, which Mrs. Pruitt had only done because the ghost of her daughter told her to. Since Faith had not died on her honeymoon, how had she died? Or did she still live? Claire realized she would need to find out. She needed to know what happened after she left 1935. She sucked in her breath and let it out slowly, no longer able to hold off the realization of who had laid dying in her arms when she had been forced back to her own time.

"Oh, Noah!" She whimpered. Claire had no idea how she would be able to accept that he had died to save her. Not only had he jumped in front of that bullet, but he also gave her the means to kill Hank. Claire tried to remember how he could have gotten one of her hairpins.

She smiled as she realized how it happened. He had his hands in her hair during their last sexual encounter in his room at the cabin. Noah hadn't made any comment, but she could now remember him slipping something into the pocket of his pants, as he retrieved her pajama bottoms. Claire thanked fate or whatever had been responsible for him pulling that thing from her hair. Hank had been smart enough to take the hairpins from her, but he obviously hadn't searched Noah well enough.

Deciding she had spent enough time in bed, Claire moved the covers aside. She got out of bed and hesitantly pushed away from the security it offered, but she almost smiled as she took her first pain free step. Except for the past week in Faith's body, it had been over ten years since she felt so good. Claire walked into the bathroom and stared into the mirror above the sink. As her reflection stared back, she smiled at seeing her own face, something she had been unable to see in a week. How she wished Noah had been able to see that face. If it hadn't been for that one dream, he wouldn't even know what she really looked like. Claire bit her lip as her eyes threatened to fill with tears. "No!" She told herself and tried to remember it had been many years since Noah had died. If she was to move on, she had to realize that he never would have been able to be a part of her life. She tried not to admit to herself that it would have been easier to at least know he had lived on after she left.

She turned away from the mirror and walked out of the bathroom. Claire halted after a few steps as that option truly surfaced in her mind. Faith must have replaced her own conscience after Claire left her body. Faith and Noah wouldn't have ended up together, which meant that Noah would have had to move on without her. He would have had to deal with the grief of losing her. Would that have been fair? Claire stopped and stared at the floor, unable to contemplate how to feel about that. She shook her head, gnawing on her lower lip in thought.

She took a deep breath and kept walking. She emerged in the hallway and went past a few rooms, but something told her to stop about half way down the corridor. Claire stared at the door a moment before entering. She didn't know what compelled her to move forward, but she gripped the curtain separating the beds and stared down at the old woman. She didn't recognize her at first, at least until her eyes opened. The old woman smiled at her, and Claire gasped as her knees buckled. Luckily, the chair behind her caught her as she fell into it.

"Claire?" The old woman asked her.

Claire leaned forward in the chair and blinked a few times. "Faith?"

Faith Pruitt smiled and removed the oxygen mask from her withered face. "I've waited my whole life to meet you." She said slowly, taking a few breaths between words.

Claire shook her head, at first not knowing what to say. She had wanted to know what became of Faith, but she hadn't expected their meeting to happen so soon. "I was afraid you were dead."

The old lips moved up into a smile. "Not yet! I've been waiting for you."

"For me?" Claire pulled the chair closer and tentatively reached for one of Faith's hands. She was almost afraid to touch her, especially after spending a week in the woman's body. No sparks flew as their skin met, and Claire almost smiled at her own notion. She gently gripped the old woman's fragile hand in her own. "What happened, Faith? Do you remember?"

Faith looked at Claire for a moment with such fondness that the younger woman almost started crying again.

"I remember *all* of it," Faith whispered. "The time you spent with Noah…how could I forget any of that?"

Claire blushed in spite of herself. "You were there?" She whispered back.

Faith slowly nodded, the slightest of a whimsical smile across her thin lips. "I was afraid at first. It was almost like watching a movie. You had total control, but I could hear and feel everything you did." She paused as she remembered. "You almost had me fall in love with him. I felt your pain when he died…which was the exact moment you left."

Claire choked a bit at that statement, even though she knew he must have died then. "I wanted to tell him goodbye," she whispered, not bothering to stop the tears that filled her eyes.

"You did." Faith took a deep but shaky breath. "Now, Claire, I don't have much time left. I've been holding on to talk to you."

Claire held her breath, almost afraid to interrupt. Faith continued and told her all that happened after she left 1935. Faith had contacted the authorities about Hank's and Noah's deaths. She had been exonerated of any crime when they decided she acted in self-defense. She then challenged the marriage license, saying she hadn't been there let alone signed anything. Her signature had been compared to the one on the license, so the marriage had been annulled. Not that it had mattered, since Hank was dead, but even her own parents testified that the Faith they knew hadn't been acting like herself. After that nightmare ended,

Faith had nothing more to do with her parents, realizing they didn't have her best interests at heart. Having gained courage from Claire's actions the previous week, she told Janet how she felt about her. The two expressed their love for each other and were prepared to struggle on their own, but that had proven unnecessary. When Faith found out she was pregnant, they both had been a bit concerned. How could she convince Janet it had been an accident? Though the end result had benefited them both, since they discovered the true reason why Hank had wanted to marry Faith. The Pruitts had set up a substantial trust that Faith would inherit should she ever marry or have a child. The trust hadn't specified that both had to happen, so even though her temporary marriage to Hank had been nullified, Noah's child ensured her the trust. There hadn't been anything the Pruitts could do to stop the transfer, and Faith and Janet no longer had to suffer to make ends meet. They were able to support themselves and the baby. Eventually Janet came to love the child like her own, and they were a happy family.

Claire sat back in the chair with her mouth agape. "I got you pregnant?"

Faith nodded with a small smile, but she didn't speak. Claire gasped and leaned forward, taking the older woman's hand again. "I'm so sorry, Faith. I had no right. I should have been more careful." The tears surprised her, and she laid her head against Faith's side. The old woman began to stroke her hair.

"You have nothing to be sorry for. You saved us all, Claire. Don't you realize that?" Faith's soft voice reassured her.

Claire shook her head, feeling miserable. "I didn't save Noah," she muttered against Faith's hip. "I let him die."

"He made a choice to save you. I wouldn't be here now, if he hadn't made that sacrifice."

Claire raised her head to meet Faith's gaze. The old woman was right, of course. Noah loved her, and he had saved her. He had saved them both.

"It's still hard to know he's dead."

Faith caressed her cheek. "He'd be dead now either way." She looked distracted for a moment. "You should go by the house. I'm sure you want to see what happened to our portrait?"

"Your house?" She breathed. "Have you been living there? What about your mother?"

Faith shook her head. "She's been dead for many years. I've lived there since." Faith smiled. "I want you to live there now."

Claire frowned. "What do you mean? Doesn't the rest of your family live there…or Janet? What happened to your child?" *Noah's child,* she finished in her mind. Her heart ached to know that she had helped to create that child.

"Our son?" She asked with a mischievous smile, before shaking her head. "He left town a long time ago. Happily married with a son of his own. Though both he and his wife are in a retirement home in Florida. They always loved that climate. Haven't seen them in years."

Claire nodded distractedly. "What about Janet?" She asked, almost afraid to voice the question.

Faith patted her cheek. "My dear one passed on nearly a decade ago. We were happy." She focused on Claire's face. "Thanks to you, we were happy."

Claire frowned, knowing that Janet had helped mess things up for them back in 1935. As if she could read her mind, Faith shook her head. "Janet loved me, and she was jealous. She regretted anything she might have done to hurt me. I forgave her a long time ago. How could I not?"

Nodding, Claire realized that Faith was right. How could she not forgive Janet? They both loved each other and had been able to spend their lives together, and that made Claire happy. The smile left her face as tears misted her eyes. "I just don't understand how I'm supposed to go on after all this? It just doesn't seem fair. I saved you, but what about me?"

Faith smiled and struggled to sit up in bed. Claire gasped and moved to help her. The older woman grasped her by the arms and then kissed her cheek before moving to whisper in her ear. "Have faith." With that she dropped back to the bed and stared intently at her. "I want you to have my diary," she whispered.

Claire blinked a few times at the subject change. "Your diary?"

Faith closed her eyes with a nod, taking a shallow shaky breath. "I've been holding onto it for you. I want you to finish reading it. You'll find it in that drawer there."

She gestured to her right, and Claire glanced at the small table beside the bed. The table had one small drawer beneath the phone and water jug. When she looked back at Faith, her eyes were closed. Claire stared at her a moment, not believing what she saw.

"Faith?" She asked her. When the old woman didn't move, she gently pressed against her arm. Still nothing, so she spoke louder. "Faith?" When she realized that the woman had died, she jumped back as if burnt. She truly had waited for her.

Chapter 28

Once the doctor looked her over the following morning, he released Claire from the hospital. Meeting Faith and watching the old woman die still had her slightly in shock. Claire wanted to ask her so much more, but she took those answers to the grave with her. She had found the diary and run from the room, clutching it tightly to her chest. She later regretted not alerting the nurses but knew that one of them would discover her pretty soon. Faith Pruitt had lived a long and happy life, and Claire couldn't be more pleased about that.

Her parents wanted her to come home with them, but Claire wanted to get back to the apartment she shared with Stefanie. She had not been able to talk to her best friend in over a week, and she missed her. As soon as they were alone, Claire burst into tears.

"Claire, what's wrong?" Stefanie awkwardly patted her on the back. "I've never seen you cry before."

"Really?" Claire sniffed. She supposed that her life had been so much better since all those surgeries and rehabilitation never happened. "I just had a very sad dream while I was in the hospital, and I'm having trouble getting over it."

"Do you want to tell me about it?"

Claire looked at the pretty blonde for a moment. "Do you remember when we were sixteen, and I met you at our favorite burger joint?" She paused as she tried to remember the name of that place. Stefanie looked confused for a moment.

"Well, Claire, we met there plenty of times during high school. Any particular time that you want to discuss?"

Claire closed her eyes a moment and nodded. Of course, it wouldn't mean anything to Stefanie, since nothing had happened. Claire hadn't been hit by a car and nearly killed. She shook her head, not sure of what to say. "What if I told you that I had been hit by a car when we were sixteen? But then a week ago, I was able to go back in time and fix everything?"

Silence met the questions. Claire opened her eyes and met Stefanie's confused expression. "Never mind, Stef. Don't worry about it. I just had a very graphic dream." Tears rolled down her cheeks as it felt like she would explode. Stefanie frowned and placed a hand on her arm.

"No, Claire. You obviously need to tell me about your dream. What happened after the car hit you?"

Claire sighed deeply and took a deep breath. She licked her lips and then told her friend everything she remembered. Stefanie sat silent through it all. She didn't speak again until she felt certain that her friend had finished with her tale.

"So you loved Noah, and then he died in your arms?" She finally asked.

Claire opened her eyes and met Stefanie's inquisitive stare. She nodded silently, tears glistening her eyes.

"Damn, girl, no wonder you're upset. I don't know how I would handle such a dream." She sighed deeply, shaking her head in sympathy.

Claire nodded slowly, "but what if it wasn't a dream?"

Stefanie frowned. "How could it be anything other than that? Do you really believe it could have been true? Claire, I've known you since high school. A car never hit you. We have been roommates since college. How could any of that dream be real?"

Claire felt lost as she thought about her friend's questions. How could she tell her that none of that had happened until she had gone back and changed things? How could her feelings for Noah not be real? Thinking about him brought forth such deep emotions that she felt more lost than ever before. The tears consumed her, and this time Stefanie didn't awkwardly console her but instead tightly wrapped her arms around her and held her.

"It'll be OK, Claire. I promise you. Everything will be OK."

Claire tried to nod but instead shook her head. Nothing would ever be right again.

Later in her room, Claire looked around the new but familiar surroundings. The book on her bed caught her gaze, and she stared at the diary. It barely resembled the one she had first found in the Pruitts' home. That one had been locked up in a secret compartment for many decades, but this one had been touched often. Faith had obviously kept it close during her lifetime. Claire sat on the edge of the bed and ran her fingers across the cover. She hadn't opened it yet, actually a bit afraid to. She took a deep breath and flipped it open. She read the first entry and smiled, before turning the pages to the last entry Faith had written before she died…at least the first time. When she saw more entries, Claire picked up the book and placed it in her lap.

A few months separated the entries, and Claire's eyes widened at seeing her name at the top of the page.

Claire,

I have so much I want to say to you, but first off, thank you!

You saved my life, and for that I will be forever grateful…

Tears filled her eyes as she continued to read Faith's message to her. She went on to explain everything that had happened since Claire left her body. The diary went into more detail, since the younger Faith had written it down as it happened. Claire completely engrossed herself in the diary and couldn't stop reading it. Margie had made many attempts at reconciling with her daughter before she died, and Faith had finally shown mercy near the end of her mother's life. She wrote how relieved she had been to finally let her mother back into her life only to lose her a few months later. Margie had left the house to Faith, and she and Janet had moved in soon after the old woman's death. Claire cleared her throat as she read the emotion packed entry.

The final entry had been written on the inside of the back cover and had been dated just a week earlier. Claire gasped, realizing that Faith knew the exact date she had been sent back to 1935. She ran her finger over the key taped below the message before reading what it said.

Claire,

I have waited many years to meet you and that day is close at hand. I'll bet you didn't know that I've been monitoring your progress for many years, biding my time until you were sent back? Only then would you even know me. I only bore a son, but I've always felt you were my daughter. I have loved you from a distance. Thank you again for coming into my life. You saved me in many more ways than just one. Attached is a key to our house. It's yours now. May you have many prosperous years of enjoyment in it!

Yours always,
Faith

PS. Don't forget to feed my cat. Her name is Claire.

Tears streamed down her cheeks as she finished reading the message. She pulled the key free of the tape and stared at it. It looked just like the key she had possessed when she lived in that house. Claire licked her lips. Could the house really be hers? Wouldn't that have to be cleared with a lawyer or Faith's family? She didn't know if she wanted to face the portrait so soon, but if a cat could be going hungry, how could she stay away? It almost felt like Faith's dying wish, so how could she say no?

Claire left her room and then the apartment without a word to Stefanie, who had been in the kitchen at the time. Claire looked for her car, pulling from her new memories to remember what it looked like. She got inside and drove to Faith's house. Once there, she sat in her car for quite awhile and stared at it. Claire's memories of the house varied, from wanting to live there to escaping being under the Pruitts' thumb. She took a deep breath and let it out slowly as she got out of her car and approached the front steps.

Stopping at the door with key in hand, Claire wondered if she should try the lock or knock first. Faith's message hadn't given her the impression that her cat would starve without assistance, so had she truly lived there without any help? Deciding to be more polite, she knocked soundly on the door. When no one answered, she slid the key into the lock and let herself into the house.

Her breathing grew shallow to be inside again. She half expected Margie Pruitt to appear in the doorway and reprimand her. Claire looked around the foyer before walking toward the living room.

"Claire?" She hesitantly called out, half expecting the cat not to appear. Claire had the feeling that Faith had just made up the pet to get her into the house. She couldn't fathom the true reason for that, but she had the feeling that she wouldn't like it. When a cute little Siamese ran into the room, Claire sucked in her breath. "Are you Claire?" She asked the cat, fighting the unexpected tears that wanted to fill her eyes. She had cried a bit too much lately and shook her head. "My name is Claire, too. So, are you hungry?"

The little cat seemed hesitant at first, but she followed Claire to the kitchen and watched as she rummaged through the cupboards in search of food. She finally found it in the pantry and poured some into a bowl. Claire the cat began to gobble it up as soon as she placed it in front of her. Claire the woman then filled up the water dish and placed that beside the bowl of food.

She petted the Siamese before straightening and leaving the kitchen. She needed to find out why Faith wanted her in the house. Her earlier destination had been the living room, so she headed in that direction. When she emerged into the room, her gaze immediately went to above the fireplace. Half expecting it not to be there, she sighed as she saw the portrait. It still possessed its strange pull, and Claire felt drawn closer to it. She hadn't gone to the house hoping to see it and be able to touch it, but now that was her strongest wish. Maybe if she touched it again, she would be sent back and have another chance at saving Noah.

She reached for the nearest chair, when a photo album on the coffee table caught her eye.

Claire let go of the chair and sat on the floor in front of the album. She recognized the first few pictures but then immediately noticed the missing wedding photo. The newspaper clipping about Hank and Noah replaced the one of Faith's death. Claire read the article while holding her breath, not bothering to ward off the tears at reading of Noah's death. Faith had been interviewed and told the press how Noah had gallantly shown up to save her from the monster Hank, only to be killed during the rescue. Hank's death had been ruled accidental, and the authorities had looked closer into the deaths of his first two wives. A connection had been made and the police decided that he had been responsible for his second wife's death as well. The next article showed Mr. Baltimore shaking hands with the detective who had reopened the case.

Claire flipped another page to see a picture of Faith and Janet. They held an infant between them. Claire raised a hand to her mouth as she stared at the son she had helped create. "Oh, Noah," she moaned as she ran a finger lightly across the baby in the picture. She shook her head, not wanting to look further. Claire stood and again reached for the chair.

She pulled it closer to the fireplace and stood on it. As she did so, she remembered how hard that had been the first time she had stood on a chair to reach the portrait. So much had changed since then. As she thought of how hard life had been before, her hand paused on its ascent to touch the portrait. What if she undid what she had changed? Was she willing to take the chance of saving Noah but allowing Hank to live? As she stared at Faith's face in the painting, she realized she would be willing to take that chance. Her hand moved forward, and she closed her eyes as her fingertips touched the canvas.

Nothing happened. Claire let out the breath she had held and opened her eyes. "No!" She yelled and placed her whole palm to the painting. "You can't do that!" She yelled at it. "How can you mess with my life like this?" She cried before jumping off the chair and collapsing into it. She leaned forward and placed her face into her hands. "It's not fair!" She moaned before standing and facing the painting with fury in her eyes and tears running down her face.

Claire clenched her teeth and glared up at the painting. She shook her head and got back up to stand on top of the chair again. She grabbed hold of the painting and pulled it off the hook. It landed on the mantel as she jumped off the chair, and she tightened her grip on the portrait to shake it.

"Why did you do this to me? I want Noah! I need him!" She suddenly let go of the frame as if it burnt her, crossing her arms over her chest. The tears streamed down her face as she looked upward and screamed, "Noah! Come back to me, Noah!"

Her voice echoed through the empty house as chills ran down her spine. A sense of déjà vu coursed through her, and she shook her head. Claire looked back up at the painting. "Were you the only one to get a happy ending?"

"May I help you?" The hesitant male voice asked from the doorway to the living room.

Claire spun around, her emotion packed encounter making her a bit giddy. Sunlight seemed to filter from behind the man so only his silhouette appeared to Claire. She frowned as she tried to focus on his face, realizing the light came from the setting sun filtering through the window above the front door.

"I'm sorry! Faith told me to come."

The man stepped further into the room and away from the light. Finally able to focus on his face, Claire's mouth fell open in surprise. "Noah?" She stammered.

He looked equally confused as he took in the scene of her standing in front of Faith's portrait. "Claire?" He countered.

Claire nodded in surprise and shock as the floor came up to meet her.

Chapter 29

Claire groaned and placed a hand to her head, almost afraid to open her eyes. When she finally did and focused on the face in front of her, she gasped and sat up. Sucking in her breath and moving farther into the couch behind her, she shook her head.

"Are you real?" Claire asked the man, half tempted to reach out to see if she could feel him. Though he looked just like Noah, it couldn't possibly be him…could it?

He frowned and a side of his mouth moved up into half a smile. "I was going to ask you the same thing."

Tears filled her eyes at seeing the familiar smile. "Is it really you, Noah?" She wanted to throw herself into his arms, but something held her back. He had died in her arms, so how could this be the man she loved?

He chuckled. "That's my name, and your name really is Claire?" He asked uncertainly.

She frowned. "Yes, but how is this possible? How are you here?"

Noah's frown deepened. "My grandmother owns this house. What doesn't make any sense is why you're here."

"Faith Pruitt owns this house." Even as she said it, realization dawned and her mouth fell open. "You're Faith's grandson?"

He nodded. "Yes, and she died last night. My parents are at the hospital handling everything. I just flew in and came straight here." Noah paused as he noticed her expression. "What's wrong? You're not going to pass out again, are you?"

His concern made her smile. "I seem to like doing that around you, don't I?" Claire sighed as she reminded herself that her Noah was this man's grandfather. Tears trickled down her cheeks. Noah surprised her by reaching out and wiping them away, gently caressing her face. She sucked in her breath at his touch, recognizing the feel of his skin.

"How can you be here?" He whispered. "I walk in and see a vision straight out of my dreams."

Claire's eyes opened sharply. "Your dreams?"

He nodded, looking into her eyes. "They started about a week ago and didn't make any sense at first. I interacted with people I had never met before, but yet I knew them…and then I saw you, and you smiled at me." Noah paused to smile at the memory before refocusing on her face. "I looked forward to going to sleep at night, knowing I'd get to see you. We fell in love in my dreams."

He noticed the open photo album on the table in front of them. "That's my father," he said as he looked at the picture of the baby held between Faith and Janet. Claire followed his gaze and nodded. He flipped some pages and then tapped another picture, "and that's me."

She looked at the picture and smiled. The baby smiled brightly back. Tears trickled down her cheeks as Noah turned a few more pages, showing many shots as he grew up. Claire's eyes widened upon seeing a picture taken of him in a park. He played in the sand box with a little girl. She sucked in her breath. "It can't be."

Noah frowned. "What's wrong?"

Claire pointed at the girl. "That's me." She had been about five years old when the picture had been taken. Of course, she didn't remember the event. She had played in many parks. "Do you know who took this picture?"

He didn't answer at first. "That's you?" He picked up the album and held it on his lap. "My grandmother took me to the park, and she took that picture." He flipped another page and this time his eyes widened. "Is that you, too?"

Faith's message in her diary came to Claire's mind. She had monitored her progress over the years. That must also have meant that she made sure that her grandson had met her. She looked at the next picture, where she had been about eight at the time. She nodded as chills went down her spine.

"Who else did you meet in those dreams you had?"

Noah shrugged. "A bunch of people. I had this really awful man named Hank as my friend. I didn't like dreaming about him, but the dreams were so vivid. I was a PI investigating him for killing his wife. You and I worked together to find proof of the crime."

"I was in these dreams?" Claire asked, thoroughly confused. "What about last night? Did you dream then, too?"

Noah frowned as he remembered. "The last two nights were strange. I left you at this cabin we were staying in and went back to town. Hank jumped me when I got to my office. He must have used chloroform or something like that, since the next thing I knew I had a noose around my neck."

Claire listened in shock as he detailed what had happened while she had been in 1935. It felt strange to hear it from Noah's point of view though, as he described how he remembered putting the hairpin in his back pocket.

"Why did you have that, by the way?" She interrupted, unable to remain silent.

Noah shrugged and shifted positions on the couch. "Well, after you…well, after we…I accidentally pulled one from your hair and forgot it was in my hand until after…"

Claire smiled at his discomfort, clearly not wanting to tell her they had sex. She shook her head, wondering how he could have had dreams of what had happened so long ago. The smile left her face as she remembered how Faith had sent Margie dreams to tell her to rent the house. Had Noah sent his own grandson dreams of what had happened, or could it be more than that? As she stared at Noah's face, she wondered if he could be the reincarnated version of his long dead grandfather. That thought warmed her heart.

"Well, I was so shocked and surprised at what had happened, that I must have subconsciously slid it into my back pocket." Noah continued with a sheepish grin. Claire had to fight the temptation to jump into his arms and rain kisses all over his face. She nodded instead.

"And you used the hairpin to loosen the knots on your wrists?"

He nodded. "Yes, and it took forever. When Hank brought you into the room, I was so afraid he'd come over and see how far I'd gotten and take away the hairpin." He paused to stare at her a moment before continuing, "but he left without walking behind me, so I was able to keep going. It didn't take much longer to get free, and then I ran straight to his bedroom. I was so afraid I'd be too late." Noah frowned. "Hank and I fought. You got involved, and he was about to shoot you. I jumped between the two of you and then..." He paused and shook his head. "Then I woke up."

Tears filled her eyes again, and she nodded. "That's probably for the best."

His eyes narrowed slightly. "I would have liked to know how it turned out."

Claire shook her head as a tear escaped and slid down her cheek. "You got shot and told me that you would cross time if you had to so that we could be together again. You gave me that hairpin, and I killed Hank with it by shoving it into his eye." She paused to swallow the lump in her throat. "You then died in my arms."

"What?" Noah uttered in shock. "How would you know how it ended? It was only a dream ...wasn't it?"

She slowly shook her head and wiped a hand over her eyes. "No, it wasn't a dream, and I was really there. Everything you've just told me actually happened."

"But how is that possible?"

Claire smiled softly. "You truly fell in love with me in these dreams?"

He frowned but nodded his head. "Yes, I did."

"Then trust me when I tell you that it happened. I can't explain how it was possible, but we were both there. I fell in love with you, too, Noah. I loved you before I even met you."

A sense of calm seemed to pass over Noah as he moved closer to her. "I know it sounds crazy, but it feels like I've waited my whole life to meet you. Grams used to tell me stories about how someday I'd meet a girl named Claire. I just figured that was where your name came from in the dream. I grew up hearing it." He looked back at the photo album. "We even played together as kids." He said, shaking his head in surprise.

They both watched as the little Siamese walked into the room and jumped onto the chair across from them. Noah stared at the cat for a moment as if seeing her for the first time. "She named her cat after you."

"That's why I'm here. I figured she needed to be fed."

"And you knew my grandmother?" Noah asked with a smile.

She nodded and licked her dry lips. "Yes, we knew each other very well." Claire slowly reached up and touched his face. "Is she why you're named Noah?"

He nodded. "My folks told me that she insisted they name me after my grandfather. I don't mind. It's a nice name."

"Yes, it's a wonderful name," without even being aware they moved closer, Claire felt the warmth of his breath on her lips just before he claimed them. Her mouth opened in a sigh as their kiss deepened. The familiar passion ignited within her, and she wrapped her arms around him with a moan.

She silently sent Faith a thank you. It seemed Claire was destined for that happy ending after all!

Epilogue

A new wedding picture soon made its way into Faith's family photo album, a picture of her beloved grandson, Noah and his lovely bride, Claire. Before they even married, they discovered they were joint owners in the old house. Faith had put both their names on the deed before she died. The lawyers had announced the news, and it mystified everyone but Noah and Claire. Considering they had every intention of getting married, it didn't bother either of them in the least.

Claire had lived a week in the body of Faith Pruitt, and now she married into her family as the new Mrs. Pruitt. The years went by and more pictures were added to the album. First a baby boy and then a girl they named Faith. Claire and Noah were doting parents, and their love for each other grew stronger with time.

Faith's portrait continued to watch over them all, never aging or fading as the decades went by.

www.ingramcontent.com/pod-product-compliance
Lightning Source LLC
LaVergne TN
LVHW091038080826
845145LV00002B/538